the
MESSY
LIFE
of
BLUE

SHAWNA RAILEY

 YELLOW JACKET

YELLOW JACKET

An imprint of Little Bee Books
251 Park Avenue South, New York, NY 10010
Text copyright © 2020 by Shawna Railey
All rights reserved, including the right of
reproduction in whole or in part in any form.
Yellow Jacket and associated colophon
are trademarks of Little Bee Books.
Manufactured in China RRD 0620
First Edition

10 9 8 7 6 5 4 3 2 1

Library of Congress Cataloging-in-Publication Data
is available upon request.
ISBN 978-1-4998-1025-7 (hc) / 978-1-4998-1040-0 (ebook)
yellowjacketreads.com

For more information about special discounts on bulk purchases, please contact Little Bee Books at sales@littlebeebooks.com.

For Samantha Noel

When it rains, look for the rainbow.
And when it's dark, look for the stars.

For Kota Bear

Always in my heart, if no longer by my side.

And for all the girls and boys out there who know
what it feels like to lose someone you love . . .
this book is for you, too.

1

I gripped his foot tightly as I wrapped the cord around his ankle. I knew it might hurt, but that couldn't be helped. The rope needed to hold. He looked up at me, and the fear in his eyes made my hands tremble. It wasn't just the sun beating down that made sweat trickle down my back. Lifting him over the edge, I tried not to think about what I was going to do. What I *had to do*.

"Noooo!"

Startled, I lost my grip and he went tumbling over the balcony headfirst. I winced when his body hit the concrete below.

Thump.

"Mr. Bunny Boo! Noooo!" Arnie ran back into the house, screaming at the top of his lungs. "Daaaad!"

I sighed. That didn't quite go as planned, but when it

came to sibling rivalry, things often didn't. Mr. Bunny Boo was just another casualty of war. He was also my brother's favorite stuffed animal, so I wasn't surprised when our dad called me downstairs a moment later.

"It was an accident," I said before my father had a chance to speak. "I was only going to dangle him. I wasn't really going to let go. It's just . . . Arnie snuck up from behind and scared me."

Arnie sniffed dramatically, clutching my dad's leg and wiping away his giant tears. Even his little chin trembled *just so*. I groaned. Did the kid always have to be so darn cute? That wasn't going to get me any sympathy.

"March right outside and find your brother's bunny. What were you thinking, Beulah?"

Uh-oh. I always knew I was in serious trouble when my dad used my real name. But with a name like Beulah, shouldn't that be punishment enough? I should get a free pass on all minor offenses.

I hung my head as I made my way around the side of the house. There was no sign of the stuffed animal anywhere below the balcony. I searched frantically through the lilac bushes and then spun in circles, panic setting in. Where could it have gone?

"Looking for this?"

I whirled around to find Crybaby-Jared, my nemesis in

2

life, leaning against a tree with a giant smirk on his face. Mr. Bunny Boo dangled over his shoulder, the cord still tied around one furry ankle.

"Give me that bunny! This is private property, and I can have you arrested."

"Seriously? We're eleven years old. Do you know of any other fifth graders still carrying around stuffed animals?"

"I know of lots besides me. Now drop the bunny and save yourself, Crybaby-Jared!"

"Finders keepers, Beulah Warren!"

"You know darn well that *my name is BLUE*!"

I pushed off the side of the house and ran at him as fast as I could. Crybaby-Jared raced down the street toward the park. I screamed all sorts of things I shouldn't say, but he didn't stop. I hopped over a flower bed in perfect form only to trip over a garden hose. I jumped back up, now even farther behind than I was before.

"I curse the day you were born, Crybaby-Jared!" I screamed at the top of my lungs.

He looked over his shoulder and laughed.

Then he ran smack into a tree.

Squealing in delight, I closed the gap and caught up to him. He flopped on the ground as tears filled his eyes. There was already a red welt where his forehead had struck the tree.

"No fair! You made me hit that tree!" he whined with a trembling chin and tears now streaming down his cheeks.

"I didn't make you do anything," I said, yanking the bunny out of his scrawny little arms. "By the way," I called over my shoulder as I strolled back toward my house, "my name is Blue. Not Beulah. And don't you ever forget it."

As soon as I arrived home, I crept through the front door. I tried to be as silent as a mouse, but the creaky hinges gave me away.

"Blue? Is that you?"

I dropped the bunny on the couch and followed the sound of my dad's voice into the kitchen. There, sitting menacingly on our table, were two glasses of milk. I dropped my head against my chest. I had earned myself a ticket to one of my dad's "milk talks." That's what my brothers and I called them. Whenever my dad had something serious to discuss, he brought out the milk.

"Yes, Dad?" I asked sweetly.

"Have a seat, Blue. Let's talk."

"Would you like me to add some chocolate to your milk?" I asked. He gave me a look that said, *Sit your butt down and don't push it.* I sat my butt down.

Twenty-two minutes later, I learned three things:

    1. It is not a good idea to dangle my youngest brother's most favorite stuffed animal over our balcony,

even if he did drop my toothbrush into the toilet earlier. It tends to put everyone a little on edge.

2. The creative punishment for said crime is to spend quality time with my brother—a demanding and temperamental four-year-old.

3. My dad's "creative punishments" totally suck.

I wiped off my milk mustache with the back of my hand and put my glass into the dishwasher just as my oldest brother, Seth, flew through the front door. My middle brother, Jackson, was right on his heels.

"But, Seth," Jackson was saying, "you promised you would take me. Ever since you started high school, you never want to do anything with me."

Seth shook his head. "That's not true. I never wanted to do anything with you *before* I was in high school, either." Seth saw me out of the corner of his eye and added, "Ask Blue, maybe she'll go."

"Go where?" I asked.

Jackson looked sideways at me, his eyes all squinty and suspicious. "But . . . but . . . but she's a *girl!*"

I get this a lot. For I am, in fact, a girl—who also happens to live in a house full of boys.

"Go where?" I asked again.

Seth answered first. "Since school's starting next week,

Kanoga Reservoir is having one last fishing tournament, and I sort of told Jackson that I'd take him. I don't suppose you'd be the best sister ever and—"

"Arnie wants to go fishing!" Arnie demanded, coming up from behind me. My dad followed with a grin.

"I think that's a great idea, Blue. You can spend quality time with *two* of your brothers today."

"Aw, Dad," Jackson pouted. "I don't want to go with Blue. Her face will scare all the fish away."

"Not if they smell you first!"

"Why can't I just go by myself?" Jackson asked my dad, but I thought it would be very helpful of me to answer for him.

"Because you're only nine years old, that's why. You're not as smart or as sophisticated as me."

"Enough, you two," my dad said. "If you want to go, then you will go with your sister."

"Go fishing! Go fishing!" Arnie chanted, and I sighed. My entire Saturday was now ruined, all because of Mr. Bunny Boo. From this day forward, his name would forever be Mr. Bunny *Poo*.

After I helped my dad find all the fishing gear in the garage, I pulled a shirt over Arnie's head and laced up his shoes. When I stood up, Arnie reached for my hand.

"Arnie's gonna catch a fishie for you," he said.

"I don't want a fishie."

"Arnie's gonna catch you a fishie."

"I don't want a fish!" I said as I tugged him out of the house and down the sidewalk. His chubby fingers wrapped around my left hand as I carried his fishing pole in my right. Jackson followed behind, still moping because Seth ditched him and he was stuck with me.

"I could've just gone alone," Jackson mumbled. "Now I'm stuck with a baby and a girl."

"Arnie's not a baby," Arnie said.

"You can't walk to the reservoir by yourself." I shook my head. "You can't even reach the top shelf of the fridge. And stop calling me a girl."

"What should I call you then? A maggot? A flea?"

I spent the rest of the walk ignoring Jackson's insults, which I could tell drove him crazy. The trail to the reservoir was only a few minutes away. We didn't even have to cross a busy street to get there. The sun reflected off the water, a bright glassy light that danced off the shiny waves. I let go of Arnie and shielded my eyes as I trotted toward a group of kids lined up. Arnie had decided about a month ago that he wanted to half waddle/half hop everywhere he went, and it made me giggle like crazy, at least when no one was looking. As he kept in step next to me, I tried to ignore all the stares and hold my head high. It wasn't my fault Arnie looked like a turkey playing hopscotch.

We'd been coming to this lake our whole lives and knew every inch of the land. Jackson quickly found his friends and stayed a good distance away from us at all times, which was perfectly fine with me.

"Arnie's gonna catch you a fishie," Arnie told me for what seemed like the millionth time, though technically it was only the third.

"Okay, Arnie. Sounds good. You catch me a fishie."

I really hoped he didn't catch me a fishie. For one, I don't like fish. They smell bad and they look funny, all bug-eyed and open-mouthed. Also, I don't like killing animals. It just so happens that I am 70 percent vegetarian, thank-you-very-much.

I found a tree close enough to keep an eye on Arnie and made myself comfortable beneath its shade. The grown-ups in charge of the tournament helped Arnie with his worms and casting while I enjoyed the lazy breeze.

I lifted my head and sniffed the air, my nose twitching like a baby bunny. I smelled everything around me: the fishy stench of bait, the pine trees that flanked me on both sides . . . and something sweet and familiar that made me smile. The scent of honeysuckle floated on the breeze, and I breathed in deep. Honeysuckle reminded me of my mother because it smelled like the lotion she'd always worn.

My mom died right after Arnie was born. My dad brought Arnie home from the hospital, but my mom stayed there for additional testing. On her way home the next day she got in a really bad car accident, and that's how she passed away. I feel bad that Arnie never even knew her. I don't know how much Jackson remembers, because he was only five years old when she died. I used to remember lots and lots, but lately it gets all jumbled up in my head. Sometimes I talk to my oldest brother, Seth, about her. He remembers things I don't—like that she hated cauliflower or how she whistled whenever she tied our shoes. I do have some memories still. I remember her smell—the honeysuckle—and her long, wavy hair and dark red fingernails.

But sometimes, secretly, I think I only remember those things because I've memorized all our photographs. Maybe I don't actually remember the real her at all.

Jackson galloped over to me with a giant grin. "Hey, Blue. Check this out." He held out a writhing snake, no longer than the ruler I used at school.

"Ew, Jackson! Get that thing away from me!" I jumped up from my comfy spot and hid behind the tree. Jackson laughed and glanced back at his friends.

"It's just a baby garter snake. See?" He thrust it toward me again and I jumped farther back.

"You are evil, Jackson David Warren! Stay away from me! I mean it!"

Jackson shrugged and made his way back toward his friends, but not before adding, "Geez, Blue. You're such a *girl.*"

"And proud of it!" I called out to his back, but he just ignored me.

He was such a *Jackson*.

For the rest of the afternoon I stayed under the tree, which just happened to be as far away from Jackson as I could get. I was relieved when a whistle blew and kids started to pack up and leave. I made my way over to Arnie and helped him with his fishing pole. He had a brown paper bag clutched against his chest.

"What is that?" I asked him.

"Nothing," he giggled, his chubby cheeks glowing red. "Just some snacks."

I knew he was up to something, but then Jackson appeared. I was still on guard. "Jackson, you better not have that snake, or else." I narrowed my eyes at him as we began the walk home.

"Relax. I let him go over an hour ago. Quit being such a baby."

"Yeah," Arnie chimed in. "Quit being a baby."

"I'm not a baby! I just don't like snakes."

"Baby," Jackson said one last time before leaving to walk ahead of us.

"Baby," Arnie repeated.

"You shut it," I told Arnie, yanking him forward to keep up. He yelped as I pulled him faster down the trail.

That night, I climbed the stairs and walked toward my bedroom at the end of the hall. I'd had enough of my brothers for the day. I tiptoed past their rooms until I reached the door with the rainbow-sparkle unicorn sticker and pushed it open.

Once inside, I was safe from anymore brotherly interactions. I sat down at my desk and brushed my hair one hundred times, so it was soft and shiny. I did this every night, just like my mom used to do. My dad said she had the softest hair in the world, softer than the softest feathers. I wanted my hair to be just like hers.

There was a light knock on my door and then it opened. My dad tripped over a pile of clothes as he came over to give me a kiss on the forehead. Our dog, Kota, trailed behind.

"Lights out, kiddo. Time to go to sleep."

"Okay. Good night, Dad."

I put the brush down on my desk and gave Kota a pat

on the head before climbing into my favorite part of my room: my bed. It wasn't just because I had a thick butterfly comforter with piles of pillows thrown everywhere; it was also because the mattress was made of memory foam and was squishy and fluffy and everything wonderful in this world. I pushed my head into the pillowy goodness and stretched my legs as far as they—

"Ahhhhh!" I screamed at the top of my lungs and flew out of bed. I was shaking by the time my dad ran into the room and clicked on the light.

"Blue? What is it? Are you okay?"

"There's something in my bed! I felt it! I think it's alive!" I'm fairly sure I looked like a lunatic.

"We'll figure it out. Don't worry," he said as the noise of doors banging open erupted all down the hallway. A moment later, all three of my brothers had filled my room.

"What's going on?" Seth asked, standing in his usual teenage attire: no shirt, boxer shorts, and gym socks. Totally gross.

My dad pulled back the top half of my covers, but there was nothing there. Then he checked the bottom part. "What in the world . . . ?"

"It's a fishie!" Arnie claimed proudly. "Arnie told you Arnie was gonna catch you a fishie."

"Dad!" I screamed, but my other brothers burst into laughter, drowning me out.

"I'm sorry, Blue," my dad said, trying not to smile. "That was very naughty, Arnie. Tell your sister you're sorry."

"But she said get a fishie," Arnie argued. "Remember, Blue? You said get you a fishie."

"Get out!" I screamed. "All of you, get out!" My dad carried the dead fish across the room as I ripped the disgusting blankets off of my bed.

"I'll get you some fresh sheets," he said, pausing at the door. I turned away. "Arnie wasn't trying to be mean, you know."

I didn't answer. I could never make him understand what it's like to be the only girl in a house full of boys and boxer shorts and snakes and fishies.

In my bed.

That night I woke up in a cold sweat, damp hair sticking to my forehead in ringlets. I kicked the covers off as I tried to catch my breath. I focused on a black dot on my ceiling, afraid to close my eyes again in case the nightmare came back.

In the dream I was little, no more than five or six years old. I'd fallen and scraped my knee in the exact same place where the moon-shaped scar I have in real life is. Was it really a dream, or could it have been a memory?

I was crying on the sidewalk, blood dripping down my leg. I heard the front door open and then someone was kneeling by my side. The scent of honeysuckle filled the air, and I knew it was my mom. I suddenly felt safe. I tried to look up at her, but the sun was shining in my eyes. I lifted my hand to shield the glare, and that's when I saw it. Her face was nothing but a blur of shadows and shapes.

I couldn't remember what my mother looked like.

2

When I woke up the next morning, my haunting dream washed back over me in one giant wave. I shot out of bed and went to my desk, quickly grabbing a sheet of paper. I printed *Linda Warren* at the top in fancy cursive. Then I wrote down everything I knew about my mom. I scribbled frantically, as bits and pieces of what I remembered trickled back to me.

My mother used to sing me to sleep at night.

When she sang, it sounded like stars twinkling, I wrote.

My mother taught art classes before I was born.

She was an artist.

My mother was captain of the swim team in college.

She was a real-life mermaid, probably.

My mother loved to read books and would take us all to the library.

Her favorite book was Charlotte's Web.

My mother and I would sit together and watch the same movie over and over again.

Her favorite movie was The Wizard of Oz.

On and on I went, until the entire piece of paper was filled with my mom's life. In the center, I'd written one word. It was larger and darker than the rest, in all capital letters, surrounded by a wiggly box.

PHENOMENAL.

My dad didn't like to talk about my mom too much. I think it was because it made him sad. But on those rare occasions when he did, he would get a distant look in his eyes. His voice would soften, and at some point during the conversation, he would always, *always* say the same thing.

"Your mother was phenomenal."

I'd woken up that morning determined to do more than just remember my mom. I mean, anyone could do that. I realized that I wanted to know her. Like, *really* know her. I could feel her sometimes, like a breath on the back of my neck, but it wasn't enough.

Lately, it seemed like I was chasing a ghost but was getting a little farther behind every day. I closed my eyes and tried to imagine my mom, but just like in the nightmare, her face was blurry. Had it always been this way? I could just make out her eyes and nose and mouth, but everything else was like a reflection in a pool of rippled water. Instead of seeing any details, her face was a misty haze in my memory.

I opened my eyes and dropped my pen onto the desk. Despite the fuzzy vision, I felt a little better after writing down my list, at least good enough to eat some breakfast. I pulled my hair back into a ponytail and headed downstairs.

As usual, my whole family was there, with all three of my brothers slumped around the kitchen table like blobs of melted Silly Putty. The sticky syrup from Arnie's waffles dripped down his dimpled chin as he welcomed me with a smile. It took everything I had not to reach across the table and wipe it off, but my dad has a very strict rule at the kitchen table and it goes like this: KEEP YOUR HANDS TO YOURSELF. It was all on account of this one time last summer, which was all my brothers' fault.

Jackson was being his usual Jackson-y self and kept flicking his green peas at me, so then Arnie started throwing his peas at me, too. Seth lobbed a spoonful of mashed potatoes that hit Jackson in the forehead. Arnie started laughing because of the potato splatter, but because he still had mashed-up peas in his mouth, green spit dribbled out all over his chin. So Jackson yelled "Gross!" and threw his napkin at Arnie's face, which of course made Arnie cry, so I did the only thing I could think of and hit Jackson with my mashed potatoes. Except I also hit him with my spoon, but because it still had mashed potatoes on it, the spoon part shouldn't even count. But my dad, however, decided that the spoon part *did* count.

So it was all their fault that we were no longer allowed any physical contact while in the presence of green peas.

Or food in general.

Or silverware.

The smell of bacon made my stomach grumble and made Kota spin in circles around my dad. For a second, it distracted me from all the swirling thoughts about my mom, but they quickly came back. I couldn't help but wonder if my brothers were also losing their memories of her. I glanced at Jackson scribbling on his drawing pad, and Seth staring blandly at his waffles. Did they forget things, too? Or could they still see her clearly in their minds? I would never ask them, of course. We didn't discuss those sorts of things. They would probably just make fun of me anyway.

Or worse: What if they thought I was a bad person?

I debated talking to my dad, but I was afraid he would be disappointed in me. Who forgets the most important moments of their life with the most important person in their life? I was the worst daughter in the world. Tears stung my eyes, and I quickly rubbed them away.

As I watched my dad open the oven to check on the bacon, I had a sudden burst of courage and decided to tell him everything—but I needed to do it quickly, so I couldn't change my mind. It's not like he could disown me. I was his *only* daughter. I cleared my throat, unsure how to start.

"So, um, Dad?"

"Hmm?" he mumbled, shuffling to the fridge and pulling out a carton of eggs.

I didn't want him to be sad, but there was a good chance talking about my mom would make that happen. I knew that as soon as I mentioned her, he would force on his plastic smile. I call it plastic because it's fake—it doesn't go all the way to his eyes. Real happiness always shines through a person's eyes.

When I didn't continue, he looked up. "What is it, Blue?"

I stuffed down the shame of what I was about to admit and said, "I wanted to ask you . . . Well, actually, I wanted to tell you—"

"Arnie spilled his orange juice!" Jackson said, which was followed by a loud wail from Arnie.

"Arnie didn't spill!" Arnie said, now crying in full force. But Arnie *did* spill, because he was now covered from head to toe in sticky orange juice.

"Blue, can you grab the paper towels?" my dad asked, but I was already at the sink, pulling on the roll. I handed him a large wad and kept some for myself, shooing Kota out of the way so I could wipe up the puddle forming on the floor. The whole entire time, Arnie screamed between sobs, "Arnie didn't spill! Arnie didn't spill!"

"Arnie's lying. I watched him do it," Jackson said calmly, which was completely unnecessary. I mean, it was pretty obvious the kid spilled his drink.

"It's just orange juice. Everything is fine," my dad said, lifting Arnie out of his chair and carrying him toward the bathroom. "But, Arnie, do you know what lying is?" They disappeared around the corner.

This meant my dad was now out of the kitchen. This also meant that the kitchen rules no longer applied. Normally, I would take advantage and attack immediately, before Jackson even saw it coming, but this morning I just wasn't in the mood. When Jackson took a piece of Arnie's waffle and threw it at my elbow, I calmly plucked it off my arm. I mean, I threw it back at him, of course. It stuck to his forehead, which is pretty much like hitting a bull's-eye, and Seth pointed and laughed. But instead of rejoicing in the victory like I usually would, with an *In your face!* or a *Take that, loser!* I just sighed and looked away. My heart wasn't in it this morning, even if my skills were clearly on point.

Arnie followed our dad back into the kitchen, staring down at his feet and sulking.

"What's wrong?" I asked him.

"Arnie spilled the juice," he finally admitted, still not looking up. I tried not to smile at his kind of adorable pouty face.

Arnie returned to his chair and started eating his now-cold waffles and swinging his legs. Seth was shoveling food into his mouth like he hadn't eaten in days, and Jackson had already gone back to drawing, like usual. I took a deep breath and tried again to tell my dad before I lost my nerve. "So, um, Dad, I, um, wanted to—"

Beep! Beep! Beep!

The fire alarm blared, the shrill blast instantly piercing my skull. I covered my ears with my hands and my brothers did the same. My dad lunged for the oven door and threw it open. A rush of smoke billowed out, filling the room with a murky cloud. I might have coughed a tad more dramatically than was necessary as I waved the smoke away from my face.

"The bacon!" my dad said, tossing the pan on top of the stove. Crispy black strips of ash lined the bottom of the pan, all covered in a greasy goo.

I was officially no longer hungry.

"Here, let me help, Dad." I grabbed the dish towel hanging from the oven door and fanned it in front of the smoke detector, waving the smoke away. I knew the drill. My dad, bless his heart, cooked a lot for the family. This meant lots of smoke alarms blaring, blackened toast burning, and water boiling over pans.

While my dad soaked the pan in soapy dishwater, I grabbed myself a bowl and filled it with Frosted Flakes.

"Sorry about the bacon," my dad said.

I patted him on the back. "Don't be sorry, old man. We can't all be perfect at everything."

I poured some milk into the bowl and sat down at the table. Arnie already had another trail of syrup, this time running down his forehead. Once again I resisted the urge to clean his face, but seriously, was the orange juice not enough? Did he have to bathe in all his breakfast foods? I tried to tell him to wipe his face mentally. I chanted the words in my mind, concentrating as hard as I could, while drilling my eyes into his own.

Wipe your forehead, Arnie. Wipe it. Arnie, wipe forehead.

Arnie put his finger in his nose. I looked away, gagging.

Unable to communicate with my brother psychically, I decided I'd rather stick a piece of my cereal onto his syrupy face. I was making the difficult decision as to whether I should use a soggy or a crunchy Frosted Flake when Seth interrupted my thoughts.

"Hey, Jackson, don't you have a baseball game today?"

Jackson's eyes grew wide, and my dad glanced at his watch.

"We're late!" my dad cried, wiping his hands on a dish towel. "Jackson, quick! Go get changed and meet me in the car." Jackson flew out of the room, and my dad rushed to pack up what was left of his breakfast, mumbling, "I can't believe I forgot."

They were gone a few minutes later, and with them went my failed attempt at being brave enough to talk to my dad. I was so disappointed; I didn't think I'd ever be able to work up enough courage to tell him again.

I went up to my room and quietly shut the door. I pulled out my Box of Randoms—a shoebox full of my greatest treasures—and rifled through its contents: a half-empty tube of ChapStick, a clip-on feather for my hair, three jelly bracelets, my purple sparkle pen (I forgot I had that), a postcard from when Seth went to Spain for a soccer tournament, a fluff ball keychain, a deck of cards . . .

Ugh. Where is it?

I started to get nervous until I finally found it buried at the bottom of the box, hidden underneath my favorite bookmark.

I picked up the bottle of nail polish and studied the color. It was a dark red, less like a tomato and more like a really ripe cherry. There were sparkles floating around inside, and I gave it a little shake, watching the flecks dance inside the bottle.

I found this nail polish years ago underneath my dad's bathroom sink and took it, knowing it belonged to my mother. I was positive my father would have given it to me if I'd just asked him, but I didn't. I just grabbed it. At the time I didn't want anyone to know I had it, and for reasons even I can't explain, I still didn't want anyone to know.

Once, I painted one of my toenails with it. Just one. It was the second toe on my left foot. I didn't want anyone to know, so I went around wearing socks for weeks until it finally wore off. But at night, when no one was looking, I would stare at that toe, shining red in the darkness, and I would remember my mom. It was like a secret between us, one that no one else could be a part of—especially my brothers. I mean, they would never have anything to do with something as girly as nail polish. They barely even trimmed those raptor claws they called toenails.

I very carefully opened the bottle and wiped the extra paint off the brush. My hand shook just a little as I swept the color onto my thumb. It was kind of thick, probably because it was so old, but it still spread okay. I held it up to the light and tried to ignore the paint that I'd accidentally brushed on the skin surrounding my fingernail. I needed a little practice.

Okay, I needed *a lot* of practice.

I was working through the rest of my fingernails when the door burst open. Arnie stood outside my room with his fingers in his mouth and his Winnie the Pooh blankie trailing behind him.

"Whatcha doing?" he asked.

It was too late to hide the nail polish, so I told him the truth. "Painting my fingernails. Go away."

He did not go away, which was actually not a surprise. Arnie was *always* there, like a stinky, gooey shadow. Or like gum you can't get off your shoe.

"Arnie wants to paint," he said, making himself at home. He sat on the floor next to me, taking an incredibly long time as he wiggled into a comfortable position.

"No." I finished off my pinky finger and put the brush back into the bottle, twisting the cap back on. I still needed to do my other hand, but I knew it was going to be even harder than the one I just did. I was left-handed, and when I went to use my right, I was going to make an even bigger mess of my nails. Sometimes all the girly stuff that makes us pretty isn't very easy to do.

Especially when you have no one to teach you.

"Arnie wants to paint," he said more forcefully. I ignored him, but I did let him stay, which was very nice and friendly of me.

"Looks like a tomato," he said.

"It looks like a dark red cherry," I corrected.

He cocked his head to the side. "Tomato."

"No. Cherry."

"Arnie wants to paint, too."

"No way."

"Arnie wants to paint!"

I could hear the beginnings of an Arnie cryfest coming on as I stared down at the colorless nails on my left hand. I didn't know how I was going to get the polish onto my fingernails without getting it everywhere else at the same time. I glanced at Arnie and wondered if he would do a better job than me if he tried. I stared down at his tiny, syrupy hands. Then I licked my finger and tried to rub the syrup off as I shook my head. I wasn't that desperate yet.

"Come here," I told him, and he bounced up and down with excitement. He plopped down next to Kota, almost sitting on his tail. "Hold out your hand like this." I showed him how to spread his fingers apart. "Now stay still."

It was much easier to paint Arnie's nails than it was to paint my own, and I was done in no time. Arnie was mesmerized as I started on another layer. I was halfway through when Seth came wandering into my room. I quickly hid the bottle of nail polish under my leg.

"Do *not* make yourself comfortable," I said. "Better yet, take Arnie with you on your way out."

"Chill out," Seth said, stretching out on my bed as if it belonged to him.

"Is my bedroom the new clubhouse or something? How come I didn't get a vote?"

"I was looking for Arnie."

"Well, you found him, so take him." I shooed them both with my hand. "Go ahead. Be gone."

Seth sat up. "What's that? Did you paint your nails?"

"What?" I asked, embarrassed. I tried to cover my hand, but it was too late.

"You did," Seth said, coming over to me and sitting on the floor. He smiled shyly as he reached for my hand. "Let me see."

I put my tiny hand in his much larger one and rolled my eyes. "It's not a big deal."

But it kind of was a big deal, because I had actually never worn nail polish before.

Seth ruffled my hair, which both annoyed me and made me feel special all at the same time. "Why didn't you paint your other hand?"

I didn't answer him. Instead, I got a brilliant idea. If

there was anyone who would help me, it was my big brother. "Seth? My *favorite* brother?"

"Hey!" Arnie said. "What about Arnie?"

"No," Seth said.

"But I haven't even asked yet."

"Nope. I can tell by your voice that I'm not going to want to do it, so my answer is no." He stood up and headed toward my bedroom door. I couldn't let him escape.

"Wait. I was only going to ask if you would help me with something. It's super-easy and it'll only take a minute, I swear."

"No."

"Will you pretty please paint my left hand?" I was embarrassed about the next part, so it came out much quieter. "I don't think I can do it."

"Really?" Seth brushed his hair out of his eyes as he thought about it. "You want *me* to paint your nails?"

I nodded.

He looked down at my hands again before shaking his head ever so slightly. He looked confused as he asked, "You painted them red?"

I nodded again and held my breath. Did he know why they were red? Was he remembering our mother's nails like I often did?

He shook his head again, but then scooted Arnie over

and sat down next to me with a sigh. "Give me your hand."

I wiggled happily and held out my hand, grinning up at my big brother.

"Thank you! Thank you!" I told him.

He chuckled. "Yeah, right. You knew I would say yes all along."

"Seth, paint your nails, too," Arnie said.

"I'll do yours next," I offered to Seth.

"No way."

"Why not?"

He thought about it and shrugged. "Okay, fine. But only if you paint them red." He held my gaze, and I knew then that he remembered.

Seth opened the bottle and removed the brush. "Do you remember the time," he started, "you got into Mom's nail polish?"

I shook my head. I had no idea what he was talking about.

"You were about Arnie's age, I think. She went into the bathroom and found you on the floor, painting the cabinets with one of her bottles. Red, of course." He looked at me pointedly again.

"I really did that? She must have been so mad." It made me kind of giggle, thinking I would do something so naughty.

29

"Stop moving," he told me as he worked on my thumb. "I thought she was going to be mad, too, but she wasn't. All she did was laugh and say, 'We have another artist in the family.' Then she cleaned it up, lifted you onto the counter, and painted your toes."

Seth finished painting my left hand, which now looked even better than the one I'd painted. I couldn't help but smile—a really big one, with teeth and everything.

"I didn't get in trouble or anything?"

Seth shook his head.

"How much of Mom do you remember?" I picked at a piece of carpet and tried to sound casual as I asked him. I could feel him studying me as I stared down at the ground.

"I don't know. A lot, I suppose." He sighed and pulled Arnie into his arms. "Why are you asking, Blue?"

Even though his voice was gentle, I wasn't ready to admit anything yet, especially to him. Seth was different than my other brothers; he was more special to me. It was important that he didn't think I was a bad daughter, especially after hearing a story about how nice our mom was to me.

"It was nothing." I quickly changed the subject. "How did you do at the surf meet last week?" I barely listened as he started talking about "this, like, really epic barrel."

Even though we'd talked about my mom, I wasn't sad like usual. Not only did I get to hear a fun, new story, but my brothers were actually hanging out with me. I would've bet a million dollars that they never would have done something like paint their nails, but here they were, laughing and sparkling themselves up right along with me. Plus wearing the nail polish meant we would each have a little piece of our mother with us. I loved that.

I waved my nails in the air to help them dry while Arnie insisted that Seth paint his toenails. His fat baby toes looked like wrinkled mini sausages dipped in sparkly ketchup. I was tempted to bite one just for fun, but I wasn't sure if that would go over very well. Arnie's moods tended to shift rather quickly sometimes, but only because he was so young and all.

When it was Seth's turn, he asked me to paint only three of his fingers on one hand and two on the other. It looked so cool that I wished I'd been the one to think of it first. Seth did that a lot. He had a way of making most of the things he did look cool.

When my dad got home with Jackson a few hours later, they found us spending quality time together: Seth was texting on his phone, Arnie was playing with Legos, and I was reading a book. But—and this is the important part— we were all *in the same room*. So that totally counts.

Jackson came in all blustery and yelling, "I hit a home run! You should've seen it, I knocked it right out of the—

Wait a minute. Are all three of you wearing red fingernail polish?"

We glanced down at our hands just as my dad came into the room, and I held my breath. I hadn't even thought about how he would feel seeing our nails; I'd been having too much fun with my dorky brothers. My face felt hot with shame. How could I be so insensitive? I should've just kept the bottle hidden. I would never forgive myself if I made my dad sad.

His eyes bounced back and forth as he studied our hands. I watched for any sign of sadness as I tucked my fingers behind my back. I glanced at Seth squirming uncomfortably, and in that moment, I wished I could just disappear.

My dad finally spoke. "Are those red fingernails?"

I didn't want to answer, but Seth was looking down at his hands. Luckily, we still had big-mouthed Arnie.

"Arnie painted nails," he said proudly.

"I see that." My dad rubbed his hand against his chin. "So can I have red fingernails, too, or do I have to make an appointment?"

Relief flooded through me while Arnie clapped his hands, delighted at the thought of more painted nails. Dad gave Seth a wink, which made him smile and relax.

"Paint mine, too, Dad," Jackson said, and everyone

froze. He raised his eyebrows. "What? You don't think I'm going to be the only one with boring old regular nails, do you?"

I went to my room and brought out the bottle of nail polish. I laughed as I watched my dad try to paint Jackson's fingernails. He did a terrible job, even worse than I did. Jackson and I took turns, each painting one of our dad's hands. When we finished, he looked down at his sparkling red fingertips and wiggled them. I wondered once again if it was going to make him sad, but when he smiled up at me, my heart skipped a beat. His smile wasn't plastic at all. His eyes had their playful spark, and I knew then that his happiness was real.

3

It was only the second week of school, but I was completely ready for summer vacation again. The sun was already high in the sky as Jackson followed me across the street to Kevin's house. I banged on the door, and a moment later, a skinny, redheaded kid emerged. We grinned our hellos, and with his backpack strapped across one shoulder, we headed down the street toward school. Jackson hung back, keeping his usual distance, which was fine by us.

Conversation with Kevin O'Dell was easy. We'd been best friends our whole lives. He laughed when I told him about my brothers and their shiny red nails. He bored me to tears when he told me all about his mother's quilting club. I had to hide my yawn when he started explaining the difference between batting and backing.

I checked to make sure Jackson was out of earshot before finally blurting out, "I can't remember my mom."

I was surprised at how relieved I felt the moment the words passed my lips. I think it was because I'd finally told someone. But Kevin didn't respond. He just shot me a funny look, like the one he gave me when I licked the sidewalk on a dare. "Did you hear me? I said I can't even remember my very own mother."

"I heard you," Kevin said. "I just don't know what to say."

"Do you think I'm a bad person? I mean, if there's a master list somewhere of all the bad people in the world, where do I rank? Am I somewhere between wicked witches and ant killers, or am I in serious Voldemort territory?" I held my breath, waiting for his answer.

"Of course not, dork." He pushed me into a prickly bush hugging the sidewalk.

"You're just saying that because you're all nice and stuff," I said, pulling myself out of the bush and picking the spiky leaves off my sweater.

"I don't think you're a bad person, Blue."

"Well, you're thinking *something*. I can tell."

Kevin shrugged. "I just think it's sad, that's all."

There was something about the way Kevin looked at me that made my stomach flip-flop and my eyes tear up. "Well, guess what? I'm going to learn all about her, and it'll be just like she's still here."

"How's that?"

"Well, for one thing, I'm going to study all the pictures of her I can find until I can close my eyes and see her face all by myself again. And also, I made a list of everything I know about her, like how she liked to swim and read and sing."

"You like to read, too," Kevin said.

"I know," I said with a smile.

"Do you have the list with you?"

I reached into my backpack and held out my treasured piece of paper. He reached for it and I paused, my hand frozen in midair. It was now my one lifeline to my mother, and I didn't want to let it go so soon after making it.

"Um, Blue? Are you gonna show it to me?"

I sighed before I finally handed it over. I watched him carefully as he unfolded the list and scanned down the page.

"Her favorite book was *Charlotte's Web*? Have you ever read it?" I shook my head. "Blue, you have to read that book. Do we still have time to go to the library before school starts?"

I grinned as we made our way into the school building. "There's always time to go to the library, Kevin."

As far as I was concerned, our school had the best library in the whole state of California. Maybe even the whole world. And not just because it had rows and rows of beautiful books—although that *was* a giant plus. And it's not even because it always had free bookmarks, and hot chocolate on Tuesdays, and book fairs twice a year—although I loved all of those things, too. It was mostly because of our librarian, Ms. McLeod.

The librarians I'd met—and I'd met a lot of them—were always the same: They smelled like cinnamon and when they hugged you, it felt like Christmas. Ms. McLeod was different. Where the others were toasted marshmallows and cozy sweaters and stars that winked at you in the night sky, Ms. McLeod was tinkling bells and sunlit adventures and coconuts on glistening sand.

She was as tall as the highest bookshelf, with long blond hair that she always wore down, never in a ponytail or a braid. And she had freckles all over, even on her arms and shoulders. (She wore a dress once and they were even on her knees!) She is super-lucky that she got so many sprinkles when she was born. I only have a few on my nose that get dark in the summer, but then they fade away to almost nothing in the winter. Part-time sprinkles just aren't as cool.

I think it was around second grade when Ms. McLeod started passing me books. She put books she thought might interest me aside and then showed them to me when I came to the library. I always checked them out and read them, even the ones that didn't actually look interesting at all. I would never want to hurt her feelings. Besides, it's nice to have someone like Ms. McLeod think about me enough to save books like that.

I waved to her as we walked in, the familiar book smell igniting my senses and putting a little bounce in my step. I sure did love this little place.

We made our way to the back of the room. Having mapped out the entire library long ago, I already knew the section my book would be in. I turned left at the READING IS FUN! poster and stopped at the first shelf, following with my finger as I scanned the list of last names, looking for E. B. White. A moment later, I was holding *Charlotte's Web* in my hand.

Would I love it as much as my mother had? What chapter was her favorite? Which character did she like best? I looked down at the book and fanned its pages, anticipating what it had in store.

And that's why I didn't see the most horrible boy standing right in front of me, just waiting for me to knock him down. Which, of course, I did.

"Hey! Look out!" Crybaby-Jared said in his whiniest voice. I didn't offer him a hand as he picked himself up from the ground.

"Watch where you're going," I said.

"I wasn't going anywhere, *Beulah*. I was just standing here and you ran me over, *remember*?"

For the love of blueberry muffins, why did his voice have to sound like a screeching elephant? It made me want to stuff cotton into my ears and then duct-tape them closed.

"I did no such thing, Crybaby-Jared, so get out of my way before I knock you down for real."

Crybaby-Jared looked back at his friends, and then he did the unthinkable. The unimaginable. The meanest, most awful thing a fifth grader could do.

He sang.

"Beulah and Kevin sittin' in a tree. K-I-S-S-I-N-G. First comes love, then comes marriage—"

"You shut your mouth right now, Crybaby-Jared!"

He stopped singing long enough to snicker. "I can say whatever I want. Like, remember that time in first grade when we had a field trip to the zoo and we were at the gorilla—"

I gasped. "Don't. Say. Another. Word."

" . . . and wherever you walked, the gorilla would follow you? Do you remember, *Beulah* . . . ?"

"If you don't stop right this second, you'll regret it," I said as calmly as I could. I didn't show my fear, but my insides were all jittery. I knew how this story was going to end.

". . . and the tour guide told everyone that the gorilla thought you were her baby!" He clutched at his sides while he laughed and laughed. His friends joined in.

It really wasn't so funny.

Kevin moved forward, but I held him back with my hand. We were better than this. We were too mature and sophisticated to give in to Crybaby-Jared's trap. He just wanted a fight.

"Let's go," I told Kevin. As I turned to leave, I glanced at the book Crybaby-Jared was holding. I couldn't help myself once I saw it was by Dr. Seuss.

"Can you even read that book? It must have a lot of big words in it."

"Very funny, *Beulah*. I'm getting it for a friend." Except he looked like he was lying, because his eyes went all shifty when he said it.

Instead of responding with one of my snappy comebacks, I decided to stick to my original plan and just walk away. And Kevin and I really were going to leave. We were already halfway down the aisle.

But then Crybaby-Jared said this:

"Blue the bluebird likes to eat worms, don't you, Baby Bluebird?"

And then Crybaby-Jared did this:

He marched down the aisle, grabbed Charlotte's Web *out of my hands, and slammed it on the ground.*

Look, it was one thing to tease me about Kevin. Or to tell everyone about the time I was mistaken for a gorilla baby. Or to say I like to eat worms, even though I totally don't. But taking his hatred of me out on my mother's favorite book, which was innocent and never did anything to anybody, was going too far. I picked that precious novel up, readjusted its jacket, and then hit him upside the head with it.

Not my best idea, no. And I'm not making excuses, but I didn't even hit him that hard. Like, if I did it to Arnie, he probably wouldn't even cry.

But because his name is Crybaby-Jared, and not Poetry-Reading-Jared or Apple Pie-Eating-Jared, he did what he always does.

He cried.

What a surprise.

Ms. McLeod stepped from around the corner at the exact moment of impact. She must have been triggered by the sound of Jared slamming the book down in the first place. I heard a gasp, followed by "Blue! What are you doing?"

"She hit me!" Crybaby-Jared's finger trembled when he

pointed at me. It wasn't shaking out of fear but because he was still crying. You know. Like a crybaby.

"Blue? Whatever would possess you to do such a thing?"

I knew she was waiting for me to explain. And I really, really wanted to tell her. *Ms. McLeod, I would say, I am defending the honor of your books. I am saving the weak from the strong. I am preserving the safety of the library.*

I am a bibliophile superhero.

Unfortunately, I live by a strict set of rules, and one of the most important rules is this: NO ONE LIKES A TATTLETALE. There are obviously exceptions to this rule. Like if someone is getting hurt or is bleeding. Or if you see an armed robbery. Or if someone takes the last piece of cake even though it's your birthday, so you should be the one who gets the last piece.

So when Ms. McLeod asked me again, "Blue, why did you hit Jared?" all I could say was, "I'm sorry, Ms. McLeod."

Crybaby-Jared's fake tears suddenly dried up. "She is a hoodlum, Ms. McLeod. You don't know her like I do. She is an evildoer who likes to—"

"That is enough, Jared. I am perfectly aware of what kind of character Blue Warren is. Do you need to see the nurse?"

Crybaby-Jared had the nerve to act like he needed to think about it. "I don't think so."

Ms. McLeod nodded once with pursed lips. "Very well then. Perhaps it's better if you went to class." She turned to me, and I could see the disappointment in her eyes. "Blue? Come with me." She sounded sad when she said it, which made me feel sad, too. "You too, Kevin."

We followed her out of the library and down the hall. It was empty now that the school day had officially started, and I was grateful that no one was around to watch my walk of shame. I wasn't surprised that we were heading toward the principal's office.

"I'm sorry I have to do this," Ms. McLeod said. I felt my chin start to tremble, so I put my finger on it to try and hold it still. "This school doesn't tolerate that kind of behavior, even if 'this school' thinks you must've had a reason to hit that boy on the head. . . ." She looked at me, and I knew she was trying again to get an explanation, but I didn't say anything. *I'm a bibliophile superhero!* I screamed inside my head. She just sighed. "Very well. I just hope you understand."

I understood. But it still didn't feel good.

When we got to the principal's office, she waved us toward the chairs that lined either sides of his door. Kevin and I sat side by side while she knocked, then went inside. A few minutes later she emerged with Mr. Nelson by her side. Mr. Nelson was short and wide with a full head of black hair. He looked funny standing next to my tall, thin, sun-kissed librarian.

Ms. McLeod gave me a wink before leaning down and saying, "Come see me before you go home today. We just got in a brand-new book that I think you'll love."

I nodded and tried to smile, but it was kind of wobbly. She gave my shoulder a squeeze before leaving us to face Mr. Nelson, our normally-friendly-but-looking-rather-annoyed-at-the-moment principal.

Mr. Nelson cleared his throat. I was perfectly aware that there was no need to do so and this was a signal for me to look at him. And I really would have, except there was suddenly a most fascinating pattern on the carpet that demanded my attention.

"Beulah?"

"Huh? Yes, Mr. Nelson?"

The principal was holding his door open. "Why don't you and Kevin join me in my office? I know you know the way." I continued to avoid his eyes as I did what he instructed.

There was a stack of photos on the corner of his desk, with one of a chubby-cheeked toddler on top. He looked like he was covered in spaghetti.

"Is that your grandson?" I asked politely, pointing at the photo.

"What? Oh, yes. That is Adam. He just turned two." He

reached for the pictures. "This is Adam at the zoo," he said, pulling another photo out of the stack.

"He's super-cute," I said. "Do you see him often?"

"Yes, my daughter and son-in-law live close by. They come for dinner every Sunday."

"That's wonderful," I said a little too enthusiastically. I needed to keep him talking. It was part of my plan. "What did you have for dinner last Sunday?"

"My wife made lasagna, and my daughter brought over some banana bread for dessert."

"Oh! I love banana bread. Does she use chocolate chips or walnuts?"

"Both," Mr. Nelson smiled. "It's my wife's recipe, actually. Handed down for generations."

"I would love to try it sometime. Do you think I could have the recipe? I'd love to make it for my brothers."

"Of course, Beulah. That is a wonderful idea."

I gave him my most winning smile. "Thank you, Mr. Nelson. And might I add that is a lovely tie you're wearing today."

Kevin sat with his mouth hanging open, so I nudged him to close it. He wasn't as familiar with this little dance as I was. Unfortunately, Mr. Nelson and I went way back.

Mr. Nelson sat up straighter, adjusting his tie. "Thank

you, Beulah." He cleared his throat. "So about this incident with a book . . . "

"I am so sorry," I began. "It's all my fault. You see, I was demonstrating for Kevin how to properly kill a spider, and I didn't see Cry—I mean, Jared—standing there. . . ." I trailed off. Even I thought my story sounded a bit ridiculous.

"Right. Well, that was very wrong of you to do, Beulah." He glanced at Kevin as though he'd forgotten Kevin was there.

"You're absolutely right," I agreed. "That's why I want to let you know that I will be volunteering in my brother Jackson's fourth-grade classroom every single day. I will help out by reading to the class during my lunch hour for the rest of the week. It's the least I can do."

No, really. It was *literally* the least I could do.

Mr. Nelson nodded. "Very good, very good. I think that is a fair punishment indeed." He stood up, and I did the same. Kevin stood as well, looking utterly bewildered.

"Thank you, Mr. Nelson, for the talk. I know I need to be more careful in the future." I moved toward the door. "Give that beautiful grandson of yours a big hug for me." I opened the door and went out. I prayed Kevin was following. If I looked back, Mr. Nelson might make eye contact and come to his senses.

I rounded the corner and let out my breath. Kevin was,

thankfully, right on my heels. "What happened back there?"

"That, Kevin O'Dell, is how you deal with Mr. Nelson. Let's just say I've had a little practice."

When the secondary bell rang for lunch, the kindergarteners through fourth graders returned to class, and all the cool older kids like me went to lunch. I scarfed down my sandwich and chips, then headed toward my brother's classroom. When I was in fourth grade, I had the same teacher as Jackson, Mrs. Henry. She was magnificent.

"There you are, Blue!" she said when I entered. "I wasn't sure if you'd remember."

"Of course," I said. "I told you last week that I'd help."

"And a help you are." She sounded so grateful, I almost felt guilty for tricking Mr. Nelson. He didn't know that I was already planning to help Mrs. Henry. "Can you grab the book over there and start reading? I'll be at my desk grading some papers."

"Ewww!" Jackson said when he saw me. "What are you doing here? I thought I smelled something fishy."

I glanced at Mrs. Henry before I smiled sweetly at my brother. Then I made a mental note to punch him when we got home.

4

"Dad? Where's the laundry?" I yelled from my bedroom. This was the third time in October that I'd been forced to track down some clean clothes. I stood in the center of my room with my freshly shampooed hair dripping down the back of my robe. My mouth was already open and poised for a follow-up scream when my dad appeared in the doorway.

"How many times have I told you, Blue? You're old enough to do your own laundry."

"But I don't know how," I whined.

"I've shown you what to do. You're just being stubborn. If you want clean clothes, you need to go into the laundry room and wash them."

"But I have nothing to wear to the choir performance, and it starts in an hour." My dad shook his head and turned away. "And I have a solo," I yelled to his back, but he kept on walking.

I slammed a pair of dirty socks onto the bed and marched out of my room. Arnie was playing with his trucks on the living-room floor as I stomped past.

"Ew! Blue's naked!" he shouted, pointing.

"I am not. I have a robe on," I said. "I just got out of the shower. Which, by the way, is a place you should think about visiting a little more often."

When I rounded the corner and flicked on the laundry-room light, I almost fainted. The largest pile of the dirtiest, nastiest clothes I could possibly imagine was stacked up as high as my neck.

"Dad!" I screamed in a panic. He came rushing in.

"What? What is it?"

I pointed at the mound of filth with my mouth agape. The scent of musty feet drifted over from the pile, and I quickly shut my mouth. "It's . . . It's . . . "

"It's a pile of dirty clothes?" my dad finished. I nodded numbly. "That's because I'm on strike."

I tore my eyes away from the clothing and looked at my father, horrified. "What are you saying?"

"I'm saying, Beulah Warren, that I am no longer doing the laundry for everyone in this family. You and Seth are old enough now. You need to start doing your own."

I blinked in confusion. Was he serious? I looked back at the stack and shook my head. "But I don't have any clean clothes."

"Well then, you better get moving."

"No, Dad, you don't understand. I don't have any clean . . . you know . . . *clothes*."

Now it was my dad's turn to look confused. "What are you trying to say, Blue?"

"I don't have any clean underwear!" There. I said it.

My dad put his hand over his mouth. I had a pretty good idea he was trying to cover up a smile, and this only made it worse.

"It's not funny!" I stomped my foot in protest.

"You're right, it's not. So you better start washing some clothes." And with that, he left me standing in the laundry room, surrounded by the filthy stench of my disgusting brothers.

I kicked a pair of muddy shorts in protest and they flew against the wall. I sighed. Might as well get started.

I went back to my room and scooped up a pile of clothes that might have been taking up residence in a dark corner of my room for longer than Arnie'd been alive. I searched under my bed and in my closet for any strays and then headed back down the hall. There was a rumbling sound, and the closer I got to the laundry room, the louder it became.

"Seth, what are you doing?" My oldest brother slammed the washer door shut and spun around. He was in his daily uniform of boxers and gym socks.

"Laundry," he grunted.

"I know you're doing laundry, but why? You barely even wear clothes."

"Yeah, well, I heard Dad telling you to do it, so I thought I should throw mine in first." He nudged me to the side as he tried to pass me, so I pushed him into the door.

"What was that for?"

"You don't even wear clothes!" I repeated louder. He shrugged and went back to his bedroom. I fought the urge to scream and kick something. Instead I decided to do the only sensible thing I could think of: I was going to tattle on him to my daddy.

In the living room, I found Dad curled up with Arnie, reading a book. Jackson was lying on his stomach on the floor, his legs in the air, watching TV.

"Seth put *his* dirty clothes in the washing machine so now I can't put *my* dirty clothes in the washing machine, and you said that I could wash *my* dirty clothes but you didn't tell him he could wash *his* dirty clothes."

Arnie glanced in my direction as I made my speech. "Blue is naked."

"I am *not* naked! I'm in a robe!" I marched into my bedroom. My inspirational kitten poster hanging above my bed shook as I slammed the door.

It was almost noon, and I needed to get dressed quickly for the performance. I grabbed an old wrinkly sundress that was crumpled up on the top shelf of my closet. I tried to smooth it out and hoped no one would notice. I put on my sparkly silver sandals and a butterfly headband. There was just one thing missing in my ensemble. A rather important thing.

I quietly opened my bedroom door and peered around the corner. All clear. I tiptoed down the hall and into Jackson's room. When I pushed the door open, I immediately crinkled my nose. Jackson's room always smelled funny, like a mix of dirty feet and mashed potatoes. I passed his desk, which was covered in paintbrushes and baseball equipment, and tried not to knock anything over. I kicked a dirty sock out of the way as I crept toward his dresser, and then I slowly opened the top drawer. There, folded neatly in a row, was Jackson's colorful display of underwear.

I closed my eyes and took a deep breath. When I opened them, I jumped. Seth was staring at me from the doorway.

"Whatcha doing, Blue?"

"Looking for my . . . my . . . pencil," I said.

"A pencil?"

"That's right. You use them to do homework." I spoke really slow. "Homework is this thing that teachers give you at school. School is this place where you go to learn things. Learning is—" I didn't need to finish, because Seth rolled his eyes and left.

I quickly grabbed a pair of underwear and was about to hurry out of the room when I noticed a brownish spot on the back of the underwear. I unfolded them and groaned. There were skid marks on his tighty-whities.

Gagging, I threw them back in the drawer and grabbed another pair. I checked them again for stains, and sure enough, there they were. Gross! Finally, the next pair appeared to be clean. They were blue with red elastic at the top. There was also a big image of Superman across the butt. I slammed the drawer shut and raced out of there.

Inside the safety of my own room, I pulled up the thick cotton briefs. Our dog, Kota, sat by my bed, watching me. He tilted his head and whined.

"Don't you judge me," I told him.

I wiggled my way down the hallway, adjusting one last time. I sat with Arnie until the rest of my family appeared and it was time to go.

The school was packed with cars. My dad dropped me off at the front of the building so I could hurry backstage while he found a place to park.

"Break a leg, kiddo," he called through the open window.

I ran into the school and headed straight for the music room. I made it just in time to follow the others single file into the theater. We waited behind the curtain for the teacher to maneuver us into our spots on the risers. I took my place next to Kevin.

"Are you nervous?" he asked. I knew he was referring to my solo.

"No," I answered, but I could tell by his face that he knew I was lying.

Tonya Morgan, the real-life true soloist, came down with the flu last Thursday. Mrs. Hall, our choir teacher, called me into her classroom and asked if I would like to sing her part. I said yes, of course! This was my one chance to show the world that I could sing just like my mother. And also a secret part of me deep down inside was hoping that wherever my mom was, she'd be watching. I wanted more than anything to make her proud. I was determined to be phenomenal, just like her.

Only now, as I stood waiting for the show to start, I was getting more and more nervous. Like pee-your-pants nervous. I could hear the sounds of families and friends taking their seats on the other side of the curtain. There was light chatter, babies crying, the squeaky sound of chairs sliding, the rustle of paper. The louder it got, the more I had to use the bathroom.

I raised my hand.

"Yes, Blue?" Mrs. Hall asked.

"I need to go to the bathroom." I heard Crybaby-Jared snicker from the bottom row of risers, but I ignored him.

"Right now? Why didn't you go before?" I didn't know what to say, so I didn't say anything. Mrs. Hall sighed. "Hurry up. Be back here in one minute."

I nodded as I shot off the platform and raced down the hall. After relieving myself, I yanked my brother's underwear up, washed my hands, and huffed back to the stage. I didn't even stop to dry my hands. I just shook them as I ran.

I landed back at my spot next to Kevin just as the curtain was being drawn. He shook his head and smiled as we started the opening song, "Hakuna Matata."

Our performance was a tribute to Disney songs. I waited—not patiently—for my solo as we sang "Under the Sea," "You've Got a Friend in Me," "A Whole New World," and "Be Our Guest."

"And now a solo performance by Beulah Warren backed by the rest of the choir," Mrs. Hall announced. "This is 'Let It Go' from the movie *Frozen*."

My stomach did flip-flops waiting for my turn at the end. I joined in with the others until the final verse came. I held my head high as I maneuvered my way through the other students and off the platform. I heard giggles behind me, but I didn't turn around. I knew some of the others were jealous that I had been chosen. I wasn't going to let them stop me. I was going to be phenomenal. I had to be.

I wondered if my mom was looking down on me right then.

I gave it my all and really got into it. I *became* Elsa. I could feel ice shooting out of my hands as I waved my arms and twirled and twirled.

"Let it go! Let it go!" I sang at the top of my lungs, still spinning in all my glory. The crowd went wild. I heard cheers and laughter from the audience and even some commotion behind me. I knew I was the right choice for a solo. Maybe next time Mrs. Hall wouldn't wait for someone to get the flu before asking me to sing.

"The cold never bothered me anyway."

I took a breath and bowed. I was phenomenal, I knew it! I had never felt more phenomenal in my entire life. Then

I heard a voice above all the others, loud and as plain as day. "Hey! That's my underwear!"

I jerked my head up, but I already knew the voice. Jackson was standing, pointing at the stage. I reached behind and felt the back of my dress. The hem was tucked inside my underwear, exposing my entire backside. My backside with a giant Superman flying across my butt.

I had a sudden flashback to all my twirling onstage. I looked out at the audience, and it was like a slow-motion horror movie. Big, ugly grins and pointing fingers were all I saw. Swaying in place, sweat began to drip down my forehead. I felt like I was going to faint.

"I didn't know you were such a big fan of Superman!" Crybaby-Jared exclaimed loudly.

I turned around and ran off the stage. I didn't stop running until I was outside and the world was silent once again. It was then that I realized I'd never even fixed my fashion flub.

I yanked the dress out of my underwear and walked slowly to our car. Then I sat down on the curb and cried. I was humiliated. This was the worst thing that had ever happened to me. I could never go to school again. I needed to move to a different town. I needed to change my name.

Well, I needed to change my name either way.

A few minutes later, I heard my family coming toward me. Jackson was still complaining that I'd stolen his underwear.

"Those were my favorite ones," he was saying. "She ruined them. I can never wear them again. They touched her butt, Dad!"

"That's enough," my dad said firmly as he came around the car. He saw me sitting there and crouched down next to me.

"That was some performance," he said quietly. My eyes filled with tears again. "You okay?"

I nodded. "I've always wanted to try boarding school," I told him. "In Switzerland."

He held out a hand and pulled me to my feet. "Come on, kiddo. It's not that bad."

"It's way worse for me," Jackson huffed. "You stole my lucky underwear!"

Seth whacked him on top of his head. "Shut up," he told him, holding the car door open for me. I climbed in. "Dad's right. No one will even remember by Monday."

I knew he was lying, but I appreciated the effort. My dad started the car and we headed home, visions of Superman swirling in my head.

"That was a *super*-good performance, by the way," Seth

said. I elbowed him hard in the ribs, but he only laughed. "I didn't know you were such a *super* singer."

"Super-duper!" Arnie shouted.

My dad grinned. "You really did a *super* job, Blue," he added with a glance in the rearview mirror. I looked away, but not before he saw my smile. "Wasn't she *super*?" he asked Jackson.

Jackson folded his arms across his chest. "I'm still *super*-mad that she stole my underwear."

"Super-duper!" Arnie shouted again.

"I'm *super*-ready to go home now!" I finally said. Seth snorted and my dad threw me one more smile and a wink.

5

I pulled the pillow over my head the instant I woke up. It was going to be the worst, most terrible, most horriblest day of my life.

Today was Jackson's tenth birthday.

It wouldn't really be so bad, normally. A little cake. The kid gets some presents. All the usual stuff, blah blah blah. Except this year, this most terrible and horrible year, my brother was having a sleepover party. That meant there would be ten obnoxious, smelly nine-year-olds ruining my entire life.

I tried to roll out of bed, but my foot got stuck on the sheet and I tumbled face-first onto the carpet. I stumbled back up and kicked out of the blankets trapping my leg.

Great. Jackson's birthday had barely begun and it was already taking over, sending me bad luck.

I padded down the hall and flopped down on the

couch, rubbing my cheek where the carpet had scratched my delicate, princesslike skin. I grabbed the remote and immediately put on my favorite TV show, *Family Tree*. It starred London Malloy, my favorite actress in the whole wide world.

Halfway through the episode, Jackson entered, followed by a sleepy Arnie. Jackson practically sat on Kota when he bounced onto the couch and ripped the remote control out of my hand.

"What are you doing?" I demanded. I tried to grab it back, but he was too quick for me. Arnie giggled and clapped his hands at the fight that ensued.

"It's my birthday!" Jackson cried. "I get to watch what I want!"

"I don't care if it's the Queen of England's birthday, you are not changing that channel." I lunged on top of his bony little body and was *this close* to getting the remote back. Unfortunately my dad walked into the room before I had a chance to retrieve it.

"What is going on in here?"

"I was watching TV, minding my own business, when your son came in and tried to change the channel."

"It's my birthday. I should get to watch whatever I want," Jackson demanded.

"Queen of England!" Arnie shouted.

"No more TV," my dad said. "Go do something else."

I stomped back to my bedroom and slammed the door. Jackson was such a baby. I stayed in my room for the rest of the morning, reading a book, until my dad called me downstairs. He looked like he'd been attacked by a party monster—he was buried underneath piles of colorful decorations.

"Can you do me a favor, Blue?" He pointed to a large helium tank he'd rented from a party store. "Can you start blowing up the balloons?"

I grabbed a pair of scissors and cut about twenty or so strings to tie on the ends. Then I rifled through the bag of balloons and pulled out all the pink ones. Jackson hated the color pink. And even though my dad always said "revenge is a dish best served cold," I disagreed. In Jackson's case, I thought it was best served *pink*.

"I still think you should have hired a clown," I said.

"Very funny, Blue. You know how scared Jackson is of clowns."

"Is he? I totally forgot." I tried to sound innocent, but I don't think it worked.

When I finished with the balloons, I helped my dad hang streamers. We twisted the brightly colored paper from one end of the dining room to the other. Balloons were tied to chairs and on the mailbox in front of the house. I had just started some music when the icky-sticky guests began to arrive. I was already at the top of the stairs, ready to hide, when I heard the most awful sound on the planet.

Crybaby-Jared's voice.

I ran back down the stairs so fast that I fell down the last three steps. I didn't care. I brushed myself off just as Crybaby-Jared entered the hall.

"Thanks so much for having me, Mr. Warren," Crybaby-Jared was saying in his nasally voice. When he saw me dangling from the staircase, he gave me a smirky grin. I wanted to slap those freckles right off his smug little face. Instead, I whined almost as bad as him.

"What is Crybaby-Jared doing here?"

My dad looked confused. "Jackson invited him to the party. I thought you knew?"

"I did not know," I answered, with my hand on my hip. "I was not informed that the enemy would be inside my house."

"Blue, that's not how we speak to our guests."

"That's because he's not a guest. He's a Crybaby-Jared!"

I turned away and marched up the stairs before my dad could say anything else. I rounded the corner to my room, and there stood Jackson, with two of his slimy friends beside him.

"You!" I pointed at him like a crazy woman. "Why did

you invite Crybaby-Jared?!" My finger was shaking.

"Jared and I happen to be great friends."

"Now I know you're lying, because Crybaby-Jared doesn't have any friends!"

Jackson took a step forward. "Maybe I am. Maybe I invited Crybaby-Jared as a birthday present to myself. Maybe I just wanted to see the look on your face when your greatest enemy spent the entire day and night in your house."

I lunged at him, but he dodged me and hopped down the stairs, followed by his two goons.

"I'll get even with you, Jackson! You wait and see!"

He waved without even glancing back.

I slammed my door and paced around my room. Oh, this meant war! Crybaby-Jared in my home? How did something like this even happen?

It took me almost an hour to muster up my nefarious plan, but as soon as I did, I ran across the street to Kevin's house. I needed some serious reinforcement, and I knew Kevin had the goods.

"Hey, do you still have that clown costume from Halloween a couple weeks ago?" I asked him in the way of a greeting.

"Yes, I think so. Why?"

"I'll tell you on the way. Where is it?" I pushed him back inside his house and followed when he led me to a large closet at the end of the hall. He rifled through a couple of boxes while I spilled the details of my revenge.

"I don't know, Blue. What if we get in trouble? What if my mom finds out?"

I waved away his concerns with a flip of my hand. "Just do it, Kevin. Remember that time Sophie Dean Thomas pushed you down the slide and you fell down and landed on your hand? Who was the one who poked her in the eye after?"

"You," Kevin answered with his eyes cast down.

"And that time we were at the petting zoo and the goat started eating your sweater? Who was the one who pulled you away from that ravenous animal?"

"It tore off half my sweater."

"But I saved your arm, didn't I? That's the important part, so you owe me."

Kevin shook his head, but I knew I had him. We chose a time and made a pact to meet later that night. Then we shook on it with the triple-slap-elbows-knock-two-fisted pinky swear. The most sacred pinky swear of all.

I could hear Crybaby-Jared cackling like a hyena downstairs, and it made my skin crawl. I shook off the chills his voice gave me and tried to concentrate on more pleasant sounds. Like nails on a chalkboard. Or a baby's shrill cry. Or a metal fork scraping against a glass plate.

Seth passed by my bedroom and poked his head in. "You locking yourself in here all night?"

I nodded. "Where've you been?" I asked him.

"Around," was his only answer. I heard his bedroom door close a moment later. I thought about asking him to help, but I was afraid he would try to talk me out of it.

Around nine o'clock, I heard the beastly boys file into the family room and set up their sleeping bags for the night. Jackson had picked *The Avengers* for the movie, and when I heard the familiar music start, I knew the time had come. I left to meet Kevin outside.

Only, once I was out there, he was nowhere to be seen. I thought we'd agreed to meet by the big rosebush next to my mailbox, but he wasn't there. The moon was full, but it was still dark out. A chill ran down my spine, and when an owl hooted in the distance, I jumped. I glanced toward Kevin's house and was about to cross the street to get him when something grabbed me from behind.

I whirled around, ready to punch the ghost in the face and run inside my house. But what I saw next was so frightening, I couldn't have screamed even if I'd tried.

Kevin was dressed up in his clown costume just like we'd talked about, but his makeup was something straight out of a horror movie. Long, sharp teeth leftover from what must have been a vampire costume complemented the blood dripping down his chin perfectly. They gave it just the right touch of creepiness. I was about to tell him when thunder boomed in the distance.

I looked up at the sky, and a fat raindrop slapped against my forehead. "Quick! Your makeup will smear!"

We ran into my house and softly closed the door. When he smiled at me, I shivered. The bloody grin was evil and dreadful and absolutely perfect.

"You. Are. My. Hero."

"Are you sure your dad won't get mad?" Kevin's nervous energy was bringing down the overall creep factor. I had to keep him calm.

"It'll be fine. It's just a harmless prank." I wasn't so sure. "We do stuff like this all the time." Total lie.

"Okay. If you say so."

He followed me toward the family room, and I motioned for him to wait there. I crept down the hall, stealthlike and slow, and peeked around the doorway. The boys were lined up on the floor like a pack of greasy sausages. They had their backs to us, so I gave Kevin a thumbs-up. We booked it to the other side of the room.

Once we reached the storage closet, I followed Kevin into the darkness and quietly closed the door. I could vaguely make out his shadow when something behind him suddenly moved.

"Kevin?" I whispered. I felt him start to shake next to me, and then I knew. . . . We weren't alone.

"Kevin?" I whispered again, softer this time, but he still didn't say anything.

I backed away fast and knocked into the door behind me. I turned from the door and bumped into something soft. Was that Kevin?

And then I heard the breathing. Kevin's. Mine. And most definitely someone else's. I was turning to leave when a hand reached from behind and covered my mouth. I tried to scream and struggle, but they had me pinned against the wall.

"Don't move," a gravelly voice whispered in my ear. I could hear Kevin fighting with someone else in the darkness, and suddenly I couldn't breathe. We were going to die. I knew it. Seconds before I was about to pass out, the light flicked on, and where there should have been only one clown, there were now three.

"Seth?" I mumbled against a white-gloved hand. He slowly moved it off my face. "Are you crazy? What are you doing in here?"

"It looks like I'm doing the same thing you're doing." He grinned.

Seth's clown face was even scarier than Kevin's. Seth nodded to the other clown—his friend Ty—and Ty released his hold on Kevin. My heart was still pounding in my chest, and I felt like I was going to be sick.

"You almost gave me a heart attack," I whispered angrily. "Why didn't you say something?"

"I didn't want you to scream. We worked really hard on these costumes."

I began to relax as my good fortune finally sank in. *We now had three clowns.* There was a very good chance that we would make Jackson pee his pants. Like, actually pee. Whiz down his scrawny little leg.

"What's your plan?" I asked Seth. "We were just going to jump out and scare them."

"Same here."

"What if we split up?" Kevin asked.

"What do you mean?"

"One of us chases them one way, one of us chases them the other way, and one of us blocks the door."

"I like how you think, Kevin," Seth said. "You take the door," he told Ty. "Kevin and I will do the chasing. Are you ready?" We all nodded.

"Wait. What do I do?" I asked. Seth laughed.

"You have the most important job of all. Here." He handed me a tiny camcorder. "Take the video."

"Big brother, I have never loved you more."

I turned the camcorder on, then snuck out of the closet and hid behind the couch, just out of view but close enough to see all the action. I hit RECORD just as the first clown tiptoed out. Seth made his way toward the half-wits still sprawled out across the floor. Thunder shook the windows, and at that exact moment, Seth the Clown pounced on the scrawny little toads.

The room erupted in screams, and I had to contain my laughter in order to keep the camera from shaking. The boys jumped out of their sleeping bags, running away from Seth—and right into the arms of Kevin. He beamed his evil smile and they retreated, but Seth was blocking the way they had come. The boys moved as one terrified herd of sheep toward the doorway, but Ty stood in front of the only exit out of this nightmare.

Then Crybaby-Jared lived up to his name. He immediately began to cry.

Jackson finally noticed me in the corner, where I was watching it all go down with the camcorder still recording. He stopped screaming and stormed over, ripping the camera out of my hands.

"You think this is funny?"

"Yes. Yes, I do." I spun just in time to dodge his punch and then Seth was by my side. Jackson scooted away from his clown face.

"Don't be mad at Blue. It wasn't all her idea."

"You ruined my party!" Jackson spat.

"You invited Crybaby-Jared!"

Jackson was about to say more, but when he turned around, he stopped. The clown masks were now off, and most everyone was laughing and high-fiving. I guess being scared half to death makes you really happy to be alive. Crybaby-Jared, for obvious reasons, was not laughing. And neither was Jackson. I watched as Jackson rejoined his group of guppies and tried to go along with it, even though he was still staying clear of the other two clowns. He tried to laugh and smile with the rest of his guests, but it looked wobbly and forced.

I quickly checked his pants, but there were no pee stains. Oh, well. There was always next year.

6

Every Saturday morning I woke up earlier than the rest of my family to watch a new episode of *Family Tree*. It's about a girl named London Malloy whose mother dies, so she and her brother go to live with their two uncles. I loved it so much. I was positive it was about her real life, too. London Malloy was the name of the actress—and the character on the show. That couldn't be a coincidence.

I always wondered how it must be for London Malloy to pretend that she lost her mom on a television show after losing her in real life. I was pretty sure I couldn't do it, but London Malloy was such an amazing actress, she could probably do anything.

Also, I knew we would be best friends if we ever met.

I mean, she had a brother and I had a brother—well, three brothers. But we were both in fifth grade. We both liked the color red, and we both liked pizza. She had a dog on the show, which meant she probably had one in real life—and I had a dog, too. Plus, we both had dark brown hair.

But the most important thing of all was that she understood my entire existence. She was one of the few people who knew what it was like to lose your mom. To have to live without her for the rest of your whole life. Not a lot of people could say that.

London Malloy was my true kindred spirit.

I was so tired from the night before that I almost slept through the season finale of *Family Tree*, which would've been soul-crushing in every way. This is because my dad came up with a new game last night after dinner. I called this one: EVERYBODY PICK UP YOUR STUFF RIGHT NOW BEFORE I BREAK MY NECK.

It's not as fun as it sounds.

I did learn a few things, though. For instance, I have a *lot* of shoes. It also turns out that I very rarely put any of those shoes away . . . and I take them off *everywhere*. It was like an Easter egg hunt without the chocolate or jelly beans. Instead, my prizes were crusty old socks and an unusual number of pebbles that get caught in my shoes during recess.

Anyways, I'd barely managed to wake up in time to watch London Malloy and *Family Tree*. Nervous that I'd already missed the beginning, I quickly flipped on the TV. When I heard the familiar theme song, my body relaxed with relief. I curled up in a blanket and bounced my feet to the beat of the music.

By the time the first commercials started, I was good and hungry. I jumped up to grab a Pop-Tart, but I never made it to the kitchen. Instead, I froze in place when the most glorious news came out of my television.

The TV show was hosting a nationwide contest.

The grand prize winner would go to Los Angeles next summer.

The grand prize winner would visit the set of *Family Tree*.

The grand prize winner would meet London Malloy!

I snatched up the remote and raised the volume, jumping up and down, trying not to scream. It was a dream come true. I had to win. I would do anything to win.

How could I win?

I took some deep breaths so I could try to calm down and focus on what they were saying. It was simple, really. To enter, I needed to draw a picture of my family and mail it in. I scrambled for a piece of paper and quickly wrote down the address displayed on the screen.

Pop-Tart long forgotten, I barely paid attention to the rest of the show. Instead, my mind raced with all the possibilities. I had to win this contest. If I met London Malloy, my life would be complete. We were destined to meet. We were fated to be friends. No—*best* friends.

As soon as the episode ended, I ran straight to my room. I pulled out my Mom List and read again the part about her being an amazing artist. She could draw just about anything: animals, people, mountains, and beaches. She was a phenomenal artist.

Phenomenal.

I wanted more than anything to be phenomenal like my mom, and this was my chance at a do-over. I could finally forget my solo singing debacle. Not only did I have the opportunity to win a trip to meet London Malloy, the greatest actress ever, but I also had another shot at making my mother proud. I needed this more than anything. I had to make this happen.

It didn't take long to realize that I had a lot of work to do. After drawing and erasing and sketching my family for more than an hour, Arnie looked like a potato and Seth's head was as big as his entire body. Jackson looked like a toad, so I obviously drew him perfectly, but the others definitely needed some help.

I made my way downstairs and found my dad sitting at the kitchen table, his reading glasses dangling from his nose as he read a thick book. I bumped into the table when

I flopped down on my chair, sloshing his coffee all over the place.

"Blue, be careful," he said, shaking the hot liquid off one of the pages.

"I'm sorry," I said quickly. "But I need your help with something." Before I could finish, Jackson came into the kitchen, his hair sticking up and his face all groggy with sleep.

My dad raised his eyebrows at the same time his mouth twitched. "Rough night there, Jacks?"

Jackson rubbed his eyes and yawned as he sat down at the table. He didn't spill our dad's coffee, which was just luck, if you ask me. I turned my attention back to Dad. "As I was saying, I need your help."

My dad looked over his glasses at me. "Okay. What do you need help with?"

"I need to learn how to draw our family, because there's this contest and it's really, really important that I win." Jackson's head shot up and he suddenly looked alert. I ignored him, like usual. "So I was wondering if I could take a drawing class."

My dad shrugged. "I don't see why not. We can look into signing you up for a class at the Art Institute. Your mom used to teach there after Seth was born, and Jackson's taken a few classes there as well."

I bounced up and down in my seat. My dad grabbed his coffee and held it off the table.

"Can we sign up today? Like, right now?"

My dad chuckled. "I doubt they have a class today, but let's go online and look at their schedule."

"I need to take a drawing class in the next eight days. My picture needs to be postmarked by December twenty-second, which is the Monday after next weekend. Do you think we can find a class before then?"

"What's this for again?" my dad asked, but I was already running out of the kitchen and into the office. I turned the computer on and waited impatiently for it to boot up.

"You're never going to find a class in the next week," Jackson said, leaning against the doorway with his arms folded like he knew everything. Which he did not. Why did he even care in the first place?

"You don't know."

"Yes, I do know."

"No, you don't."

"Yes, I do," he said. "And if you do find a class, it'll probably be all filled up anyway."

I didn't look at him. I refused to stoop down to his level and continue to argue. He needed to understand that I was much older and much wiser than him. I didn't have time to bicker with such an immature child.

"If you don't leave, I'm telling Dad!" I said with just a hint of a whine.

He shook his head at me as he left, but I didn't care. I was incredibly determined. A few minutes later, I was scrolling through a list of classes on the Art Institute's website. There was one class that looked perfect. It was called Life Drawing, and it was next Saturday. That would give me a day and a half to finish my family portrait after the class. I would still have time to mail it in before the deadline.

I needed to take that class.

I showed it to my dad, who agreed that it did, indeed, sound perfect. There was just one problem. When he tried to register me, the website said there were no more spaces available.

My eyes filled with tears, but I tried to hide it. I didn't want my dad to think I was overreacting, but I could barely contain my disappointment. It felt like all my hopes and dreams were going up in a ball of flames.

It didn't really matter anyway, I told myself, trying to get a grip on my tears. I mean, who was I kidding? I could never win a drawing contest, even if I took a thousand art classes. I wasn't phenomenal at anything, but I was especially not phenomenal at drawing.

I thanked my dad for trying and went up to my room.

I closed the blinds in my window, blocking out all the sunshine and happiness. I climbed onto my bed and stared into the darkness. After a few minutes, I opened the blinds again and let the sunlight back in. It's easy to ignore the things that sparkle if you only focus on the things that dull your shine. Even feeling as sad as I felt, I never wanted to ignore the sparkles.

On the following Monday at school I tried not to think about London Malloy or the contest or disappointing my mother. Instead, I tried to focus on the things I was really good at. I found out that I am actually very talented at:

> Getting to school late
>
> Doodling hearts on my math homework
>
> Avoiding Crybaby-Jared at recess
>
> Spelling the word *hippopotamus*

When I got home, I dropped my backpack in the hallway. Then I picked it up and put it where it was really supposed to go, which made me quite proud of myself; I'd remembered for once. I was so busy giving myself a mental pat on the back that I didn't even notice my dad sitting on the stairs. He had the phone in his hand.

"I just got off the phone with Tamara Jenings. She's the director of the Art Institute and used to work with your mom, so I called in a favor. It seems they are willing to overlook their strict class sizes and allow you to attend that class on Saturday, if you still want—"

I ran to my dad and hugged him as hard as I could. "Thank you, thank you, thank you! I'm going to go get ready!"

I hopped over him and raced up the stairs toward my bedroom. My dad hollered at my back, "Get ready for what? You still have the rest of the week!"

I sat at my desk and made a list of all the items I needed to bring with me to class. It wasn't a very long list. I chewed on the top of my pencil while I tried to think of everything. Sketch pad. Check. Pencil. Check. Eraser. Check.

On Tuesday, I collected the items I'd put on the list and put them in a brown paper bag.

On Wednesday, I watched back-to-back reruns of *Family Tree*, which was very inspirational to me artistically.

On Thursday, I tried sketching just my dad, but he ended up looking like Jack the Pumpkin King. (On a side note, it turns out I can draw a pretty decent Jack the Pumpkin King).

On Friday, I paced back and forth all afternoon after school, waiting anxiously for Saturday to finally arrive. That's when my dad pulled me aside.

"Blue, you're driving us all crazy. Can't you find

something else to do besides walk back and forth past my office door?"

"I'm sorry, I don't mean to. It's just that I'm so excited for my art class tomorrow."

My dad stood up from his desk, snapping his fingers with a mischievous grin. "I have an idea. Follow me. I have something for you."

I followed him into his bedroom and waited while he rustled around in his closet. He came back out holding a navy-blue corduroy bag with two brightly colored birds stitched on the front.

"This belonged to your mom. We bought it on our honeymoon in Italy. She actually embroidered it herself." He ran his hand lightly across the fabric before unzipping the main compartment. "She carried it to every single one of her art classes. It's the perfect size to carry a sketch pad and plenty more." He held it out to me. "She would want you to have it for your class tomorrow." He tried to smile, but it was obviously plastic.

I took the bag from him and stared down at the two birds. I didn't know how to explain to him how much it meant to me, so I didn't say anything. But I think he knew. He pulled me in for a hug and I buried my face into his sweater. He smelled like peppermint and soap. For a second, I didn't want to let go.

I finally found the words to say: "I love it."

"Go on," he said, letting go and ruffling my hair. "Get outta here and fill that bag up with all your art stuff."

I peeked over my shoulder as I left the room. My dad's plastic smile was already beginning to fade as he picked up a photograph of my mother. I closed the door quietly.

7

By the time the art class finally arrived, my stomach was tangled up in knots. I held tight to my special art bag, now filled with my very own sketch pad, my black-and-white-checkered pencil, and my favorite strawberry-scented eraser. I tried to pretend like I wasn't scared, but the truth was that I was terrified. I wasn't afraid of the teacher or anything; I was afraid I would be a disappointment. I mean, if my mom was an artist, that should mean I have the same talent, too, right? Maybe my drawing skills were just buried deep down inside me, far, far away, miles below the surface, so small they were barely even there. But they *were* there. I had to believe that.

I'd told my dad that I could walk to the classroom on my own, but once I got there, I wondered if I'd made a mistake. Being so close to Christmas, the temperature had dropped, and I used that as an excuse for the chills I suddenly had. I pulled my sweater tighter around me as I entered the classroom. The class was crowded, and when I scanned the room, I realized immediately that it was full of adults—there wasn't another kid in sight. I checked the room number one more time; it still read 308. This was definitely the right room.

I entered as quietly as I could. I think if I could have made myself invisible, I would have. I wiped my sweaty palms on the front of my jeans and tried to stay calm. The tables were pushed together to form one large circle, with everyone facing toward the center. I found a spot near the far window and quickly sat down.

The teacher still hadn't arrived, so the students stood chatting with one another, sipping on their teas and coffees and looking very sophisticated. I hadn't thought to bring anything, but watching them sip on their hot drinks made me suddenly thirsty. Which then made me suddenly hungry. Luckily for me, there was a basket of fruit in the middle of the circle. I glanced around the room before helping myself with a shrug. *First come, first serve,* my dad always says.

The shiniest apple ever created sat inside the basket and was calling out my name. It was buried underneath an orange and a pair of bananas, but I wasn't going to let that stop me. I nudged it out of its little tunnel and licked my lips in anticipation. Then I spilled every piece of fruit stacked inside the basket all over the floor in one giant rush of *noooo*!

So much for being invisible.

I didn't look at anyone as I grabbed as many pieces of fruit as I could and shoved them back into the basket as fast as possible. I crawled underneath a table for the last one—a kiwi—and then placed it carefully on top.

I sat back down, still too afraid to look anyone in the eye. I'd managed to save my shiny red apple, and when I bit into it, the crunch was so loud, it sounded like I'd used a microphone. I sat a bit lower in my seat. A man in a green coat—the kind that looks like it belongs with a suit—was watching me from across the room. He looked angry. I shrugged and pointed at the rest of the apples in the basket. If he wanted one, he could just get up and get one. Sheesh.

I reached into my bag and pulled out my pencil. Might as well be ready for when class started. I couldn't help but overhear the two women sitting next to me while we waited.

"Beth Ann told Tabitha that the last time she took this class, they used a live model."

"Is that so?" the other woman asked.

"It is. Did I also happen to mention he was nude?"

I accidentally inhaled part of my apple. I began to choke, holding on to the table as I coughed and gasped for breath. Eventually, with the help of a very nice stranger who patted me on the back, I coughed out the chewed-up piece of apple. It flew out of my mouth and across the room, landing on the table in front of the man in the green coat.

Oops.

He looked disgusted. I shrugged and tried to give him a smile, but he rolled his eyes at me and looked away. If we were getting graded in this class, I would already have a big fat F, and the class hadn't even started yet.

Just then, the teacher entered the classroom in a dramatic flourish, waving her arms about as she spoke. She introduced herself as Cosimia and told us her name meant "of the universe." And that she was. She gave us a long speech about freedom of expression and how society tries to make us "color inside the lines." And it seemed like the more she spoke, the crazier her arms got. By the end, she had broken out in a sweat and strands of her curly hair were shooting away from her head in a frizzy disaster.

It was quickly obvious that everything Cosimia did was going to be the same way: completely over the top. Some of her words were exaggerated and drawn out; others were barely whispered. She wore a long, flowy gown that billowed behind her wherever she went. She was like a real-life rainbow.

She was like art itself.

When she paused to catch her breath, I took a bite of my

apple, the crunch echoing in the brief silence. She whipped toward the basket of fruit in the center of the room so fast, her dress spun into a blur of painted waves.

"My dear, what is it you think you're doing?"

Her eyes bored into my soul. I glanced to either side of me, then back at Cosimia. She was still staring at me, her left eye twitching as she waited.

"Um, are you talking to me?" I said, not very loudly.

"Of course I am talking to you. Who else would I be talking to?" She spun in a circle, gesturing with her hands to the other students. I'd never seen anyone with that many rings on their fingers. And they were so large. She had a giant red gem on her middle finger that reminded me of my perfect apple.

The apple!

Oh, no.

I looked down at the half-eaten piece of fruit and gulped. "Do you mean, why am I eating this?"

"That is precisely what I mean. My dear, do you know what that is?"

I was so confused. "You mean, besides an apple?"

"That"—Cosimia pointed with a bejeweled finger—"is my warm-up."

"Your . . . *what*?"

"My warm-up. I put that basket of fruit there for my

students to sketch at the beginning of the class, before we start on the real assignment."

"But I thought this class was supposed to teach us how to draw people?" I hoped I didn't sound rude.

"It is, it is." More hand-waving. "But I always start my classes with a warm-up." She leaned over me, her wild hair tickling my cheek. "Today, you *ate* the warm-up." She didn't give me a chance to apologize. She gave me a smile and a wink, then spun around to talk to the man in the green coat.

While she was distracted, I snuck back over to the basket and buried my apple underneath the other fruit. It was mostly hidden except for a corner of it, and that part of the apple didn't have any bite marks on it, so the warm-up was practically the same as before.

Cosimia started the class with her fruity warm-up and made us all sketch the basket of food while classical music played in the background. I'd only sketched the top of one banana when my pencil broke. I raised my hand.

"Yes, my dear?" Cosimia asked.

"I broke my pencil." I held up my special checkered pencil to show her.

"It seems you have. Pencil sharpener is over there," she told me with another exaggerated wave.

I quickly sharpened my pencil, then went back to

drawing the fruit. When I finished both bananas, I moved on to the kiwi, now dented a bit because of my earlier spill. I was so wrapped up in what I was doing that I didn't even notice the man who'd quietly slipped into the classroom. It wasn't until Cosimia started moving the basket away that I realized what was happening. My heart pounded in my chest.

The man was wearing a white robe.

And Beth Ann told Tabitha that the last time she took this class, they used a live model.

And he'd been *nude.*

The two gossiping women sitting to my left fidgeted in their seats when they noticed him making his way toward the center of the circle of tables. I surveyed the room, and it seemed that I was the only one who was concerned with what was about to happen.

Look, I have three brothers. And I've seen Arnie naked a thousand times. But I was *not* okay with a nude model. I was trying not to panic, but it was obvious that everyone else had forgotten I was even there.

With the fruit gone, the model leaned against the now-empty table in the center. He was reaching for the belt securing his robe.

For the love of onion rings, I had to put a stop to this.

"No! Wait!" I yelled, standing up. "I don't want to see

you naked!" I covered my eyes with my hand. "Don't do it!"

"My child, what on earth are you talking about?" Cosimia sounded so taken aback that I peeked through my fingers. The model's hands were frozen on his belt, and Cosimia was staring at me, horrified. A hum started to fill the room as everyone began murmuring to one another. I slowly brought my hand down away from my face.

"I thought . . . I mean . . . he's wearing a robe. . . ."

Cosimia waved her hand at the model and he pulled off his robe. He was wearing a white T-shirt and shorts.

Oh.

That was awkward.

I shifted uncomfortably and I could feel my face turn hot. A buzz erupted all around me and a few people chuckled, which made me feel even more embarrassed. If every set of eyes hadn't been glued to me, I would've gladly crawled under the table. Forever.

"May we continue, my dear?" the teacher asked. I nodded.

For the next ninety-five minutes, Cosimia walked us through different drawing techniques. I gave her my undivided attention as I tried to take in what she was teaching us and apply it to my hand, but unfortunately my hand wouldn't cooperate. When I told it to draw a circle, it drew an egg. When I told it to draw a full head of wavy hair, it drew Medusa. (On a side note, it turns out I can draw a pretty decent Medusa).

So, I wasn't surprised when, as Cosimia circled the classroom, she paused, standing behind me and leaning down low so as to see my drawing in even more detail. Great. I knew she was silently judging my artistic abilities, but there wasn't a whole lot I could do about it. I swallowed the lump in my throat and reminded myself that this dreadful class would be over soon.

And with it would go my chances of ever winning the contest. But I couldn't think about that now.

The sleeve of Cosimia's dress brushed against my hair as she straightened, but not before whispering in my ear, "I see a great deal of potential in you, child. You aren't afraid to color outside the lines. The greatest artists never are."

My mouth hung open, I was so surprised. Could that really be true? I wanted so much to believe her. I hunched over my drawing, now more determined than ever to get the hands I'd been working on just right.

At four o'clock sharp, the class ended. I packed up my things and waved goodbye to Cosimia. She waved back, her hand flowing as if guided by the wind. I smiled to myself on the way out.

My dad was waiting in the parking lot, and I rushed to his car. I slammed the door and laid back in the seat, my eyes closed.

"Everything all right?" my dad asked.

I took a deep breath as I tried to decide whether or not I liked the class.

"I do not color inside the lines," I said, feeling just a hint of pride.

My dad started the car and chuckled. "Oh, I know. You never have."

As soon as I got home, my brothers gathered around and asked to see my drawings. It caught me off guard and made me feel kind of shy, which was odd, because they were only my brothers. I mean, most of the time they smelled like moldy cheese, for goodness' sake. So what if they were giving me a little extra attention, right? We always enjoyed Seth's surfing competitions and Jackson's baseball games. It felt good to have them take an interest in me. I took a deep breath and pulled out my sketch pad, opening it up on the kitchen table. I hoped they didn't notice my hands shaking.

Jackson pointed at my first drawing. "Hey, isn't that the lady who has snakes on her head instead of hair? What's her name?"

"I don't know who you're talking about," I said quickly.

"You know who she is. If you look into her eyes, you turn to stone."

"Medusa," Seth said.

"Yes!" Jackson said. "You drew Medusa."

I flipped the page, trying to look cool. "Yeah. It's no big deal." But it was a big deal to me, because I hadn't actually drawn Medusa. I tried to stay calm.

The next page was a pair of hands clasped together. I thought I'd done a really good job on them, so I stood a little taller.

"What's that?" Arnie asked, pointing at the hands.

"Boxing gloves," Seth told him without any hesitation.

"No, I think they're clams." Jackson tilted his head. "Or wait. Is that a dragon?" I thought Jackson was trying to be mean, except there wasn't even a hint of a smile. He looked genuinely curious.

I took back my sketchbook and stuffed it into my bag. All three of my brothers looked surprised.

"What'd you do that for?" Seth asked. "We weren't finished looking."

"Arnie wants more!" Arnie said, pounding on the table.

I was already strapping the bag over my shoulder so I could hurry up to my room. "I'm just tired and hungry, that's all. I want to put my stuff away so I can eat."

I marched up the stairs, now frustrated with the entire day. Cosimia was wrong. There was no potential for greatness when it came to me and art. I was beginning to think I would never be phenomenal at anything.

I got my piece of paper out of its hiding place and made myself comfortable on my bed. I reread everything I'd written down about my mother.

Singer.

Artist.

Swimmer.

Mother.

Phenomenal.

I took a quick shower and got ready for dinner. I'd just put on my most fluffiest socks when I heard a quiet knock on my door.

"Who is it?" I called.

"Jackson."

Ugh.

I swung open the door and glared at him. The last thing I wanted to hear was that I was too stupid to draw. Or that I looked like a donkey. Or that I was a complete failure at everything I tried and that I would never be as good as our mom at anything because she was phenomenal and I was just a mediocre eleven-year-old girl with no special talents of her own.

Or whatever else Jackson would come up with.

"What?" I snapped, my guard on high alert.

"Here. I wanted to give you this."

He held out a piece of paper, and I took it from him. When I saw what it was, I gasped.

"Jackson! Where did you get this?"

"I drew it." He went over to my dresser and began fidgeting with a box of hair ties.

I was staring at a portrait of our family, and I was amazed by all the detail. It was . . . beautiful. Our dad was in the center, with Seth holding Arnie on one side and Jackson and I on the other. He even drew Kota lying near our feet. But the very best part of the whole thing was our mother. She was draped in a yellow fringed dress, with a matching yellow feather in her hair.

"Um, Jackson?" I tried to ask gently, "Why is Mom wearing a feather in her hair?"

"Because she always wore them."

"No, she didn't."

"Yes, she did. She's wearing one in the photo Dad keeps by his bed, so she obviously liked them."

I tried not to smile. Our mom hadn't gone around wearing feathers in her hair all the time. That photograph was from a costume party our parents had gone to. I glanced at his drawing again. Now I loved it even more *because* of the feather.

"It's amazing, Jackson. Really. You definitely take after Mom." At least one of us did. I was trying not to feel jealous when something occurred to me.

"Wait a second. There is no way you could have drawn all of this in one day. When did you do this?"

Jackson shuffled his feet. "I saw the commercial for the *Family Tree* contest a couple of days before you mentioned it. I know how much you love the show, so I was going to enter for you."

I couldn't believe it. Who was this imposter and what had he done with my brother? The look on my face must have shown what I was thinking.

"Whatever. Just take the thing." He thrust the portrait at me and turned to go. I glanced at the sketch again. It was more than just amazing.

"Hey, Jackson."

"Yeah?"

I swallowed the lump in my throat. "This drawing is phenomenal."

Jackson beamed. "You think?"

I nodded. "Absolutely. And I know Mom would've thought so, too."

It crushed me inside, but in that moment, I knew what

I wanted to do. I went over to my desk and emptied out the beautiful art bag Dad had just given me. "I want you to have this. It was Mom's, and she kept her art supplies in it." I held it out to him, but he just gawked at me like it was some kind of trick.

"Why are you doing this?" he asked.

"Why did you draw this picture for me?"

He shrugged. "Because I'm better at drawing and I wanted you to have a shot at winning."

"Well, I'm giving the bag to you for the same reason. You're the best artist in the family, Jackson, not me. You deserve to have something special of Mom's." Something occurred to me. "And look! It has two birds on the front, so they can remind you of the feather in Mom's hair."

Jackson slowly took the bag from me, his eyebrows raised into arches. "You don't have to do this," he said shyly.

"I know. But you didn't have to draw that picture for me, either. Besides, I think Mom would want you to have it."

"You really like the picture that much?" He was beaming, and I couldn't help but smile back.

"I already told you. It's phenomenal."

8

I gathered up my babysitting bag and slung it over my shoulder. It was heavy with the weight of four books, two movies, one craft project, and a stuffed otter I'd named Ollie.

"I'm leaving, Dad," I called as I bounded down the stairs. I had one foot out the door before I heard my dad yell.

"What time will you be home tonight?"

"Mr. Salazar will drive me home around nine o'clock."

"Remember to lock the doors when they leave."

"Yes, Dad."

"And don't forget to—"

"Yes, Dad."

"And call me if you need—"

"Dad! I'm babysitting down the street. It's not like I'm going to Argentina or something." I kissed him goodbye and skipped out the door. Two minutes later, I was hurrying up the Salazars' driveway, ready for an evening of fun.

Mrs. Salazar answered the door in a flowing green dress. They were going to a New Year's party tonight, and she looked fancier than I'd ever seen her. She flipped her hair to the side as she greeted me in a hug.

"There you are, Blue. I was just getting ready to call you. Delaney's in her high chair, just finishing up her spaghetti. You know the drill: Our numbers are on the fridge, and Mrs. Edgerly is next door if you have an emergency."

I followed Mrs. Salazar into the kitchen and froze when I saw Delaney. Normally, she is the cutest little two-year-old you've ever seen. She has wavy brown hair and the most adorable dimples you could imagine. When she smiles, she wrinkles her nose and covers her mouth, and I just wanted to squeeze her—but right then all of that was forgotten. Delaney was covered in red spaghetti sauce and plastered all over with pieces of noodle. They were stuck to her forehead, arms, legs, and nose, and it looked like one was growing out of her ear. Who knows? Maybe it actually was.

Mr. Salazar came into the room dressed in a suit and tie. He laughed when he saw his daughter. "Did she get any food into her mouth?" He bent down to kiss her, but when he couldn't find a clean spot anywhere, he gave up and patted her head. Then he washed his hands with extra soap.

"Do you think you could give her a bath tonight, Blue?

Normally I wouldn't ask, but, well, as you can see . . ."

"That's fine. I don't mind at all."

Mr. and Mrs. Salazar exchanged a look. "There's something we should warn you about. Delaney is . . . how should I put this? Going through a phase," Mrs. Salazar said.

Mr. Salazar added, "It seems like every time she takes a bath lately, she . . . well . . ."

"Sometimes she needs to go to the bathroom."

"Oh." Gross. "She pees in the water?" I asked.

"Well, not exactly." Mrs. Salazar looked uncomfortable. "She actually tries to poop."

I swallowed. "She poops in the bathtub?"

"Well, she tries to. If you watch her, you can pull her out fast enough and put her on her potty. She usually stands when she needs to go, so just keep an eye on her. If she stands, that's your warning."

"It's really important that she doesn't go potty in the bathtub. If she does, it's a whole mess. You have to take her out, clean up, put her back in, and start the whole thing all over again."

I glanced at little Delaney, swinging her chubby legs in her high chair and flinging noodles all over. It was going to be a long night.

"Got it. Give Delaney a bath, but don't let her go number two in the tub."

Ewwww.

The Salazars left, and for the first time ever, I was a little nervous to be alone with Delaney. With sauce all over her, the sweet little girl that I usually enjoyed babysitting now resembled a demon child . . . who evidently pooped in her bathtub.

I sat down next to her and picked up her spoon to help her actually get some of the food into her mouth. We were on our third scoop when she flung a handful of sauce-covered noodles at me. One of them hit me in my eye.

"Okay. We're finished here," I told her. She giggled while pounding her fists on the tray. I quickly grabbed her plate and placed it in the sink before she could knock it over. I turned back to the high chair—keeping an eye on the demon child—and took a really deep breath. How was I going to get her out of that contraption without getting covered in spaghetti sauce?

I found a towel in the linen closet and crept back toward the kitchen. I wrapped myself in the towel and then reached underneath Delaney's arms to lift her out of the chair. I held her away from me as I sped down the hallway toward the bathroom. I sat her in the empty bathtub, clothes and all.

"Bath bath!" she squealed. "No clothes!"

I helped her remove her messy clothes and threw them, inside out, in a pile on the floor. I turned the faucet on and she played in the rushing water. When the temperature was perfect, I sat on the floor next to her.

I sang "Rubber Ducky" and even made up a cute little dance to go with it.

She splashed me in the face for my effort.

We played with some cute plastic dogs that I found lined up along the edge of the tub. I arranged them from smallest to biggest and gave them sweet little names.

She drowned them.

We played dolphin and mermaid. I was the dolphin, and she was the mermaid. I moved my hands like they were a fin and saved the mermaid from an evil stingray.

She thanked me by deciding mermaids like to cook dolphins.

I made lots of bubbles with a bubble wand and soap. They bounced in the air as I blew them toward the bathtub.

She tried to eat them.

Finally, I shampooed her hair until there was no more sauce to be found. She tilted her head back and I used a large plastic cup to rinse the soap off. I was turning around to reach for the bottle of conditioner when I felt warm liquid being poured over my head.

I screamed like a giant baby.

"What the—?" I spun around and found Delaney standing in the bathtub. She had leaned over the edge so she could pour an extremely large cup full of water over my head. She was still holding the cup and laughing her little butt off.

"That is not funny, Delaney!" The water dripping down my back made me shiver. "That was not very nice!" She wiggled around, doing what looked very much like a victory dance.

"Wa-wa-water! Wa-wa-water!"

"Look, Delaney. I'm going to go get another towel. Stay here." I backed out of the bathroom and rushed down the hall to grab a towel from the closet. I was back in literally two seconds. What happened next was *not* my fault.

When I entered the bathroom, Delaney was still standing. Only now she was standing kind of . . . funny.

"Delaney? What are you doing?"

She looked at me and then closed her eyes. Her body shook just the tiniest bit, and then it hit me. She was going to drop a kiddie into the pool. Release the chocolate. Float a sea pickle. A Winnie the Pooh-Pooh. A poop-scoopin' boogie.

I had to act fast. I rushed to the edge of the tub to pull her out, but she backed away and tucked herself into the corner. I watched in horror, knowing what would come next. It was too late. The poop would drop at any second . . . so of course I did the only thing I could think of.

I reached out, cupped my hands, and caught it.

Looking back, all I kept thinking was that if the poop landed in the water, everything would have poo-contamination. Delaney. The bathtub. The plastic toy dogs. The washcloth and the bottle of conditioner floating in the bubbles.

I should have just let her poop in the tub. Instead, hands full of her warm waste, I screamed my head off.

Startled by my outburst, Delaney began to cry. I didn't care. I dropped the turd into the toilet and flushed it immediately. Also, I kept on screaming.

Stumbling toward the sink, I used my elbows to turn the water on. I scrubbed my hands together, as fast as I could. No matter how much liquid soap I dumped on my hands, there was never enough. I scrubbed and scrubbed some more. And some more after that. Delaney continued to cry, and I thought very seriously about joining her.

When I finally felt clean, my hands were raw from scrubbing. I started to calm down. Going back to Delaney, I took the towel and dried her off.

"It's okay, Delaney. You're okay." I picked her up and held her.

She stopped crying and sniffed. "You touch poo-poo?"

Ugh.

"Yes, Delaney. I touched poo-poo."

I carried her to her room, and we sang songs as I helped her put pajamas on. Then I took her downstairs and put on a princess movie to keep her occupied while I tried to clean up the high chair area. It was a total disaster. I had almost finished wiping down the floor when someone banged loudly on the front door. Delaney was too busy playing with a plastic phone to notice. They banged again, louder.

I crept toward the door and through the window, saw the silhouettes of two very large men.

"Hello? Please answer the door!"

No, no, no, no, no. I rushed to Delaney and scooped her into my arms. My heart raced as I heard a small sound coming from her toy phone. I put it to my ear and almost dropped her when I heard, "—police should be arriving now."

"Hello?" I said into the phone. The plastic toy phone I thought Delaney was playing with turned out to be one very real phone.

"Ma'am? Is everything okay there?"

"Yes. Who is this?" What had Delaney done now?

"This is 9-1-1. I believe there are police officers already at your residence."

I plopped Delaney on the ground and, with the phone, made my way to the front door. The banging was louder and more urgent. When I swung the door open, two police officers stood before me, looking annoyed.

"Hello. We received a call. Is anyone else here?" the closest officer asked me. Afraid to speak, I just shook my head. He peered around me. "Do you mind if we come in and take a look around?" I nodded and moved out of their way. While one of the officers searched the house, the other one stayed behind to ask me questions.

"Are you home alone?"

"Yes."

"Where are your parents?"

"I'm babysitting."

"Did you call 9-1-1?"

"No."

"Well, someone called 9-1-1."

I gestured toward Delaney, who was sitting on the couch, swinging her legs back and forth and mimicking my earlier screams.

"Are you injured?"

"No."

"Is the child injured?"

"No." *Not yet.*

The other officer rumbled back down the stairs.

"I saw Delaney playing with the phone, but I just assumed it was a toy. I think she may have been the one who called." I was trying really hard not to cry. "I'm really sorry."

"Is there an adult you can call?" he asked nicely. I nodded and immediately called my dad.

My dad showed up less than five minutes later, and I was relieved. He talked for a few minutes with the police officers and then they left. But not without telling me for the fifty-sixth time how important it was not to dial 9-1-1 unless it was a true emergency. Which I already knew, because I was not the one who called.

As soon as they were gone, I called the Salazars and explained what happened. They agreed that it was better if they just came home. My dad insisted on staying with me while we waited for them, and I was secretly glad. Delaney, unaware that anything unusual had occurred, played happily the whole time. Except for when I stopped her from tearing the pages out of a book. And from hitting the family cat on the head with a blow-up beach ball. And from drawing on the wall with her crayons.

When I started cleaning the rest of the spaghetti mess, my dad offered to wash the dishes while I dried and put them away.

"Delaney never used to be like this," I told him, stretching to put a plate on a high shelf. "I don't understand why she's changing. She used to be so sweet."

"You know, I seem to remember you doing similar things when you were just about her age," he said with a chuckle.

"Jackson, too. And you were both so close in age that you were constantly getting into trouble together."

"Really?" The idea of us actually working together made me giggle with surprise. "Like how?"

"Let's see," he said, looking deep in thought. His face lit up when he thought of something. "When Jackson was two and you were three, we had a hard time keeping Jackson's clothes on. He'd take them off constantly." I snickered again. "One day, your mom looked out the window and found you with Jackson in his underwear, lying down in the grass. When she went outside, she found a bottle of baby powder you'd taken from Jackson's room and completely emptied in a pile on the lawn. You were rolling Jackson back and forth in the white powder, covering him in it. When she asked you what you were doing, you told her, 'Look Mommy! Jackson's fried chicken!'"

"I did not!" I said, shocked but with a giant grin.

"Oh yes, you did," he told me, laughing. "And another time, I found the two of you in the bathroom, flushing toilet paper. It was still attached to the roll, which was still attached to the wall, so every time you'd flush, the toilet paper roll would spin like crazy. You and Jackson just laughed and laughed. You guys thought it was the funniest thing ever."

"I never knew that!" I told him incredulously. I put the

last of the silverware into the drawer just as my dad rinsed out the sink. "Will you tell me more?"

I curled up next to him on the couch and spent the rest of the time listening to my dad tell more stories while we watched Delaney play. When the Salazars arrived home, they weren't upset at all.

"These things happen, especially when little Delaney is around." They laughed good-naturedly, and I faked a smile.

The truth was that I just wanted to get out of there and go home. I sighed with relief as my dad drove us the short distance. He must've felt sorry for me, because he even let me pick the music on the way. We'd just pulled into the driveway when he said, "I'm really proud of you today. You stayed calm and handled the situation exactly the way you should have."

I beamed. "Thanks, Dad." Then I followed him into the house and made a beeline for my bed. Even five minutes of peace and quiet would feel like heaven.

9

I opened the cupboard in the garage and took the leash from its hook. As soon as Kota heard the familiar rattle of his chain, he bounded across the room and slammed me into the cupboard door. His wagging tail made his butt wiggle like my great-aunt Martha's when she danced at my cousin Mary Sue's wedding. Except Kota had more rhythm.

After a few tries, I finally managed to clip the leash to his collar, but before he could yank me out the front door, my dad stopped me.

"Blue, why don't you take Arnie with you?"

"Huh?"

"I said, why don't you take Arn—"

"No, Dad, I heard you the first time. My brain just refused to process your request."

Arnie jumped up and down. "Arf! Take me! Take meeee!

Arnie's a doggie. Arf!" My dad gave me a *do-you-see-how-excited-your-brother-is?* look. I sighed.

"Fine. Hurry up and put your shoes on."

"Doggies don't wear shoes," Arnie said. "Arf!"

"They do when it's still winter. You don't want your paws to freeze, do you?" I crouched down and grabbed ahold of Arnie's legs. He barely sat still long enough for me to slide his shoes onto his chubby feet.

I opened the door and Kota zoomed past me, fast as a rocket ship. I stumbled off the front porch and slid across the grass. That's when I saw her.

Her is my mean next-door neighbor. Her name is Jane, and she's a witch. I say this because I'm pretty sure she cast a spell on my dad. Whenever he tries to talk to her, he kind of stutters and his face turns red. He starts running his hands through his hair and he laughs a lot. Then she'll turn her beady little eyes toward me and ask me all sorts of really suspicious questions like, "How was your day today?" or "Do you like chocolate chip cookies?" As if I would eat her poisoned baked goods.

On this particular afternoon, she was outside sweeping the sidewalk in front of her house. Her *haunted* house, no doubt. I ignored her as I turned in the opposite direction and headed down the street. Kota peed on every bush we passed. It makes for a long walk when your dog stops every five seconds to take a whiz on a lavender bush. And a pine tree. And a flower bed. And a hibiscus plant.

I was tugging Kota away from a thorny rose bush, for reasons that should be obvious, when I realized Arnie was being particularly quiet. I turned around and found him facing a tree with his pants down around his ankles.

"Arnie! What are you doing?" I yelled. "Are you crazy? You can't just pee outside!"

"Arnie is a doggie. Arnie wants to go potty like Kota."

It was like Delaney all over again! I shook my head, looking around to make sure no one saw us. I must've been cursed.

"You are not a dog! Come on. I'm taking you home."

"Arf" was his only response.

We made our way back the way we came. This time, I quickly pulled both of my "dogs" past the shrubs and greenery as I stomped down the sidewalk. When I rounded the corner, I saw my witchy neighbor, Jane, still sweeping away. Only, the closer I got, the more I realized what she was really doing. She'd swept all of the crumpled leaves and dirt and pieces of grass toward the front of my house. It was littered about the sidewalk in front of the path leading to my front door. Before I could say anything like, "Hey, lady, are you collecting herbs to stuff inside your voodoo doll?"

she'd already gone back into her house and closed the door.

I went inside my house, but it was now empty. There was a note from Dad telling me he'd gone to the store and that he'd taken Jackson with him, so I had to babysit Arnie until he got back. Seth had left early in the morning to go to the beach with his surfer friends, so he'd be gone for a little while longer, at least. After settling Arnie in front of the TV, I hung up the leash in the garage and grabbed the broom.

I let the door slam as I stomped down the path to the sidewalk. I collected every little grain of dirt I could find and swept it back to the front of Jane's house. It didn't take very long, and I was quite proud of myself as I strolled back inside. How dare she mess up the front of our house!

I grabbed a glass of water and was mid-sip when I heard a faint scratching sound coming from outside. Curious, I walked over to the window and promptly choked on my water. Jane the Witch was sweeping the pile back over to our side of the walkway! I stood with my mouth ajar as I watched her swish and flick her broom back and forth. I would've marched outside right then if not for the fact that I was afraid she might turn me into a toad. Or even worse—what if she turned me into one of my brothers?

While I waited for her to finish, I began to pace. My hands were shaking because of the obvious betrayal. It was up to me, and me alone, to protect my family. To protect our castle. To protect our rights as citizens in this glorious country, the United States of America!

But, looking back, maybe I took it too far.

Once she had finished and gone back inside, I reached for the broom and crept outside. I was relieved to find Jane's door still shut. I was afraid that she might be spying on me from one of her windows, but I was too mad to stop. As fast as I could, I pushed all of the debris right up to her porch. I also accidentally picked up her newspaper and threw it into the birdbath. Then I ran like the wind.

My heart was pounding once I was back inside the safety of my house. Arnie barely glanced away from the TV as I flew past him. I waited by the window and watched. Seconds turned to minutes, and my heart pounded in my chest as I thought of what she might do. I began to pace—it was better than just sitting there—and I couldn't help but wonder what was taking so long. I don't know how much time passed before good ole Janey-poo came outside once again.

This time, she had no broom in her hand. She pulled the sopping-wet newspaper out of the birdbath and hopped off the porch. She carefully stepped around the pile of dirt and leaves before turning toward my house.

I rushed to the side of the window and pulled the curtain shut as fast as I could. A moment later, I heard the doorbell.

Arnie jumped up and Kota began to bark wildly, but I held them both back.

"Don't answer it," I whispered loudly. "It's the witch from next door."

"Miss Jane? But Arnie likes Miss Jane. She's nice."

"No, Arnie. She only *pretends* to be nice." The doorbell rang again. "She's really a witch who eats little children." What can I say? I was desperate. Plus, technically, I didn't have any proof that she *didn't* eat kids.

She banged on the door. "Blue, I know you're in there. Answer the door. I saw what you did to my newspaper."

Arnie looked puzzled, and I shrugged. He tried to squirm to the door, but I held on tight.

"Do not answer that door!"

Then he bit me. I lost my grip long enough for him to run for it. He grabbed ahold of the handle, but by the time he got the door open, she was gone. The drippy, mushy newspaper, however, remained.

"Ew," Arnie said before scooting back to the TV. I picked up the soppy mess and slammed the door shut. I dumped what was left of the newspaper into the trash with only one thought racing through my head.

This means war.

I couldn't go into battle alone, though. I needed an army. I glanced over at Arnie, who was busy watching space aliens with his finger up his nose. I don't even think he was picking it. He was just using his nostril as a finger holder. I turned away, gagging. I needed to hold out for the heavy artillery. Luckily, I heard the garage open. My secret weapon had just arrived.

Jackson came through the door carrying half a dozen grocery bags slung all the way up both arms. "Are you going to just stand there looking ugly, or are you going to help?" he asked.

I was debating whether to punch him or tell him what had happened when my dad entered.

"Go grab the rest of the bags," he told us.

I followed my brother out and stopped him at the trunk of the car.

"I need your help, Jackson."

"*I need your help, Jackson,*" my brother mimicked in a baby voice.

"I'm serious."

"*I'm serious,*" he repeated.

I resisted the urge to deliver that punch I still owed him and said instead, "Fine. If you don't want to go to war with me . . ."

"What do you mean 'war'?" he asked, his interest peaked.

"Yeah, how are you going to war?" Seth asked, strolling

through the open garage with his surfboard under one arm. His hair was still damp and curled around his face.

Even better. Another soldier.

I explained what went on between Jane and me to my eager listeners.

"Wait a minute. She just swept all the trash into our yard?" Seth asked.

"That's what I'm trying to tell you! She is a horrible witch who sweeps dirt and eats little children."

"She doesn't eat children," Seth answered.

"But we can't let her get away with this!" Jackson added.

"So let's come up with a battle plan," I agreed. We huddled close to work out the details.

"Good night, Dad." I smiled sleepily. Or at least, I tried to make a sleepy face. It was hard to do with this much excitement blasting off inside my head. With my luck, I probably looked like I was trying not to fart.

"Sweet dreams," he added before switching off the light.

I lay in bed, watching under the crack in my door for the lights to fade. When the house was completely dark and silent, I waited another ten minutes as planned. Then I climbed out of bed and pulled my shoes on. The boys were already waiting for me by the back door.

"Did you get them?" I asked Seth.

"I grabbed every single newspaper I could find in this town." His grin was pure evil.

I'm not going to lie—I felt a pang of doubt. It wasn't too late to rethink our strategy. I was about to say something when Seth opened the sliding glass door to our backyard.

"They're hidden under the deck. Come on."

I kept my mouth shut and followed. Now was not the time to chicken out. Even Jackson was ready, and he's a whole year younger than me.

The night was cool, and a slight breeze shifted in the air. There was hardly any moon out, but lights from the surrounding houses gave us just enough light to see. I jumped when a dog barked in the distance.

Seth reached under the deck and pulled out a stack of newspapers as high as my knee. I let out a breath. That wasn't so bad. It would definitely make a mess, but it wouldn't be outrageous. I almost started to smile, but it quickly died before it had fully formed.

Seth reached back under the deck and brought out three more stacks. The gravity of what we were doing hit me. Could this be considered real vandalism? I think I threw up in my mouth a little.

"Let's do this."

I tried to shake off the feeling of dread. I watched as Jackson swallowed and nodded. I wondered if he thought that maybe this was a mistake, too? It seemed like a good idea at the time, but now that we were out here, in the night, trashing our neighbor's yard? Maybe not my brightest plan.

But it was too late to back out now. We each grabbed a handful of newspapers and lined up along the fence separating our yard from Jane's. One by one we took a sheet of newspaper and balled it up. Then we promptly tossed it into Jane's yard.

When my small stack was empty, I grabbed as many newspapers as I could carry and balled up entire sections of paper. Again and again and again . . . About halfway through, I began to relax. This was actually fun! Jackson laughed when I threw a paper ball at his face, and I dodged Seth's attack when he tried to stuff a wad down my back. We giggled under the moon as we destroyed our neighbor's backyard. By the time we finished, it looked like a newspaper factory blew up in her perfectly manicured, witchy lawn.

We ran back to the house, our hands black from all the ink. We carefully washed them in the kitchen sink, watching the dark water swirl down the drain. I gave my brothers a huge smile and a thumbs-up, then padded down the hall to my room. It took me a while to fall asleep after the adrenaline rush of our little adventure, but eventually I gave way to the sweet bliss of slumber.

I woke up to Arnie sitting on top of my chest, grinning from ear to ear. His face was covered in chocolate.

"Wake up, Blue! We have chocolate chip cookies for breakfast."

"Huh?" That didn't seem possible. "Dad gave you cookies?"

"Not Daddy. Miss Jane!" I sat up so quickly that Arnie tumbled to the floor.

Oh, no.

I took a deep breath and reminded myself that whatever punishment came next, it was the price I had to pay to protect our home. Our kingdom. Our—

I'll just stop there.

I rubbed the sleep from my eyes as I made my funeral march toward the voices coming from the kitchen. Arnie ran ahead, singing, "Blue's awake! Blue's awake!" Nothing like a grand entrance.

"There you are." My dad smiled at me. "Jane brought over some fresh-baked chocolate chip cookies. Isn't that nice?" Jane was leaning against the kitchen counter, sipping a cup of coffee. Jackson and Seth were seated at the table, each with a plate of cookies and a glass of milk. Seth looked up when I entered, gave me a *just-go-with-it* look and shrugged. Jackson's eyes were round as saucers and kept darting from Dad to Jane in terror.

I took a plate of cookies from my dad and flopped onto a chair at the table. I was halfway through my milk when Jane said, "I want to thank you, Blue, for your help yesterday." I choked on my sip and milk sprayed through my nose. I pounded my chest.

"Ewwww!" Arnie said, pointing at my face. "Blue snotted milk!"

I wiped my face with a napkin and glared across the table at Arnie. Jackson smiled at my misfortune, clearly no longer scared, but Seth still looked as nervous as I felt.

"What did Blue help you with?" my dad asked, looking from her to me.

"Oh, a little bit of this. A little bit of that. Isn't that right, Blue?" I barely nodded. "As a matter of fact, I don't know how I'll ever repay you."

"I'm sure you'll think of something," my dad said, popping one of her delicious poison cookies into his mouth.

"Yes," Jane said, looking directly at me, "I'm sure I will."

10

Once the weather finally started to warm up, Arnie was back in swim lessons. I watched as he splashed happily with the other runny-nosed kids in the pool, kicking his legs as hard as he could while holding on to the edge of the wall. I watched Kiera, the instructor for the class, work her way down the line of students, correcting their legs so they stayed straight and stiff. When she got to Arnie, he barely needed any help at all. He was like our mom: a natural-born swimmer.

My teeth were chattering now that I was out of the pool and sitting on a wooden lounge chair. I tried to stretch my towel around my arms, but it wouldn't reach. I couldn't find any beach towels before we left the house, so I was stuck using an extra-small bath towel. It barely fit around my waist.

As fascinating as it was to watch my littlest brother

put his nose in the water and blow bubbles, he wasn't the reason I'd all of a sudden started coming to his swimming lessons. At first, it was because of my mom. Knowing she was practically a mermaid made me want to be a better swimmer like her, and I knew that with practice, I could make it happen.

But then I met Kiera, Arnie's swim teacher. She was in high school and was even older than Seth—and way, way cooler. She wore her hair piled on top of her head in a bun that somehow looked messy and perfect all at the same time. She had at least ten bracelets tied around one arm, each one made of different-colored threads weaved together in intricate designs. And, even in the water, she wore purplish lipstick.

If I were old enough to wear makeup, I would wear purplish lipstick just like her.

I pulled my legs up and tried to tuck them under the tiny towel for extra warmth. I glanced down at the other end of the pool, where a diving class stood along the edge. One by one, the teacher called their names and they took turns plunging effortlessly into the deep water. If I knew how to dive, and if I were allowed to wear purplish lipstick, I would quite possibly be the coolest girl in my school.

But my lips were plain old lip color. And I was way too scared to dive.

"Yoo-hoo! Blue? Earth to Blue."

I turned to Arnie's class and saw Kiera waving at me. I sat up straighter. "Yes?"

"Will you jump in and help me for a few minutes?"

I dropped my towel and slipped into the pool. It wasn't deep; the water didn't even come up to my shoulders. Kiera handed me a green foam kickboard with a smiley-faced starfish on it. She held on to one with an orange octopus.

"Okay. We're going to have each kid hold on to the kickboard while we pull them across to the other side of the pool and back again. Do you think you can handle that?"

I nodded, afraid my voice would squeak if I tried to talk. Kiera the Kool was talking to me. And she wanted my help!

I started with Delilah, a small girl with braided pigtails. She held on to the board and kicked her legs frantically, splashing water everywhere, including into her eyes. She squeezed them shut and continued to kick like she had absolutely no control over her own legs. When we got to the end of the pool, I turned around to take her back.

"Are you Arnie's sister?" she asked me with her eyes still closed.

"Yep."

"Can I tell you a secret?"

"Um, sure," I told her.

"I eat my boogers."

I'd been watching Arnie's swimming lessons for at least a week. That was *not* a secret.

"Well, maybe you should eat a bigger breakfast instead."

When we got to the end, I helped Delilah hold on to the edge of the pool with the others and pulled the next student over to the kickboard. He was a feisty four-year-old with flaming-red hair and a face full of freckles.

"Who are you?" he asked.

"I'm Blue," I said.

"No, I mean what's your name?"

"Blue."

"That's a color, not a name."

"Well, it's *my* name," I told him.

He paused a moment before saying, "Your name isn't Blue."

"I think I know what my name is," I said, spinning him around once we got to the far end. "What's your name?"

His eyebrows knitted together as he thought about his answer.

"Orange."

The next kid up for a kickboard ride was a girl decked out in a shiny pink bathing suit.

"I like pink," she told me while she kicked her teeny-tiny legs.

"That's nice. What's your favorite food?"

"I like pink," she said again.

I giggled under my breath. "Right. Pink." We got to the end of the pool, and I said, "It's time to turn around."

"I like pink," she said.

Shocker.

By the time I brought "Pink" back to the others, Keira had announced they would each try to put their whole face into the water.

"No face," Arnie said. Booger Girl and Pink hugged each other, their eyes full of fear. A couple of the other kids looked like they were ready to cry.

"It's okay," Keira said, waving her hands. "You can still hold on to the wall, I just want you to try and put your face in. So hold your breath and close your eyes. You can do it! Just lean down . . ."

I left her to deal with the guppies and swam back to the other end of the pool. There was a group of kids tossing a beach ball back and forth, playing some homemade version of volleyball. I passed them quickly and found a quiet corner near one of the pool ladders. I leaned my back against the wall and slowly kicked my legs as my eyes drifted back toward the diving class. I really wished I knew how to dive. It would be almost as good as purplish lipstick.

I tried to memorize the way they stood at the edge of the pool and the way they tucked their hands together. I was about to practice with my hands when I heard, "Bombs away!" followed by the biggest splash imaginable. It covered my entire head, forcing my hair onto my face and into my eyes. When Seth surfaced in front of me a minute later, I wasn't surprised. I also splashed him in the face with as much water as I could.

"What'd you do that for?" I said.

"Do what?" His grin looked slightly evil.

"What are you even doing here?"

"Dad asked me to pick you guys up after Arnie's class, and since I was coming from the beach, I already had on my bathing suit. Thought I'd swim until Arnie finished."

The advanced class was still diving. I was distracted for a split second as I glanced at the next swimmer dive in. It was flawless. I bet mermaids knew how to dive. I bet my mom knew how. I looked back at Seth and found him watching me.

"What?" I snapped.

"Do you know how to dive?"

I didn't want to lie, but I was embarrassed to tell him the truth. "Everyone knows how."

"I'm not asking everyone. I'm asking you."

I shrugged. "Probably. I've just never done it before."

Seth started paddling toward the ladder. "Come on, I'll teach you."

Butterflies swarmed in my stomach, but I was too excited to care. If anyone could teach me to dive, it was Seth. He practically lived at the beach, and he was always winning surf competitions. I followed him out of the pool and stood next to him at the edge. He put my hands together and stretched them up over my head. Then he pulled my arms down toward the pool.

"Now tuck your chin against your chest like this." I did as he showed me. "Next, I want you to lead with your hands. Push them toward the water and let everything else follow. Try it."

I looked at the blueness of the water, wavy with reflections. Before I could even think about what I was about to do, I pushed off the edge toward the waiting water.

I did a perfect—but painful—belly flop.

When I broke the surface of the water, Seth was smiling. "You were so close. Try it again."

I shook my head. I was humiliated. Who knew how many of the students in the diving class had seen me? They were probably laughing at me right that second. I refused to look in their direction and find out.

"Come on, Blue. Nobody gets it right on their first try." I shook my head again and swam toward the ladder. I was done. The impromptu diving lesson was over.

"Where are you going?" I heard Keira ask. I turned

around and found her swimming toward me. "Your brother's right, you know. It just takes practice."

Seth stood up straighter and ran his hand through his hair. I looked back at Keira, and she was smiling at him, a little twinkle in her eye. I glanced toward Arnie's class and saw that they were all finished. Arnie was out of the pool and sitting on my chair, wrapped in both his towel and mine.

"Come on, Blue," Seth said. "I'll show you one more time."

I didn't want to try again, but now that Keira was watching, I didn't want her to think I was a scaredy-cat. I slowly pulled myself out of the pool and stood next to my brother. Keira got out and stood on the other side of me. They took turns giving me pointers.

"Don't look at the water."

"Pull your shoulders back."

"Lean more forward."

"Push from your toes."

I did an actual dive on my fifth attempt. It felt incredible. My hands sliced through the water and then the cold liquid rushed against my face. In that moment, I was a real-life mermaid. I'd never felt so close to my mom. I was just like her.

As I swam up toward the surface, I felt a crazy rush of

energy. I did it! I really did it! Seth and Keira were going to be so proud of me. I pulled myself out of the pool, expecting congratulations, but they were gone. I scanned the deck and found them walking together toward the diving boards. I couldn't believe they'd stopped watching me. I suddenly felt alone. Well, until I heard Arnie yell "Splish splash!" at the top of his lungs.

I watched Seth climb up the tallest diving board and puff out his chest. It was obvious he was trying to impress Keira. And it was also obvious that it was working. She gazed up at him with her hands clasped together. Dancing hearts were practically floating above her head.

I couldn't believe I ever thought she was cool.

Seth stood on the edge of the board and gave it a little bounce. I held my breath. He closed his eyes, reached his arms into the air, and after the briefest pause, he jumped. His body rocketed into the air and then, in one fluid motion, he flipped three times. Right before he hit the water, he twisted his entire body like a pretzel. There was barely a splash when he hit the water headfirst.

It was a phenomenal dive.

When Keira and Seth finished showing off for each other, Seth was finally ready to take us home. He exchanged phone numbers with Keira before they said goodbye and then whistled on the way to his car. Maybe I just imagined it, but it seemed like he suddenly had a bounce in his step.

Love is so weird. It seems like it should take you a long time to love someone, and I think, sometimes, it does. But I also think love can hit you all at once, like a lightning bolt that explodes in your chest.

"Don't worry, Blue. You'll learn how to dive someday. You just need to practice more."

I sat down in the front seat and didn't say anything. Seth hadn't seen me do it, just as I suspected. All it took was one girl in an amazing shade of purplish lipstick for him to forget all about me. It didn't feel very good at all. I stared out the window on the way home in silence.

I slammed his car door and marched up the driveway as soon as we got to the house. All I wanted was to be alone. I stomped into the house and was already heading toward the stairs when Jackson came tearing out of the kitchen like a crazy person. He waved a crumpled envelope above his head.

"You won! Blue, you won!"

I had no idea what he was talking about, and frankly, I didn't care.

"The contest! You won the grand prize! You get to visit the set of *Family Tree* and meet London Malloy!"

I froze. My heart stopped. Time stood still. Everything went black. Life ceased to exist.

"Did you hear me?" Jackson asked when I didn't say anything. "You won!"

"I heard you." I could barely breathe.

And then something crazy happened. Something I never in a million gazillion years thought would ever happen. We ran to each other and hugged. Like an arms-around-each-other-without-trying-to-cut-off-oxygen-supply kind of a hug.

It felt kind of weird, actually. Kind of like hugging a monkey, I'd imagine.

11

Kevin and I walked to school slowly, chatting away about winning the *Family Tree* contest. He was almost as excited as I was. It made me sad that he couldn't go with me, but I promised to take lots and lots of pictures.

We had always been two peas in a crazy little pod, and we shared almost everything. There was the time we pooled our money together until we had enough for one ice cream cone. (He let me choose the flavor.) Or the time we had only one pencil, so I would write a spelling word and then he would write a spelling word, and so on.

We do not, however, share a fifth-grade classroom.

I would've liked to share a classroom with him. It would've made school so much easier. It's hard navigating friendships and homework and teachers and bullies. And, of course, the reason we all go to school in the first place: the never-ending popularity contest.

Kevin and I were somewhere in the middle, which was fine by me. I wasn't as hated as Crybaby-Jared, but I wasn't as cool as Shane Butts, the star athlete, either. There was a pecking order to fifth grade, and we were all aware of where we stood. I was happy with my place in the pack.

I waved goodbye to Kevin once we got to school and headed for Mrs. Wood's dungeon—I mean, classroom. It's not that I think my fifth-grade teacher is an ogre or some kind of crypt keeper or anything. She's nice enough. It's just, she keeps all the blinds shut and all the lights off. She thinks it keeps the classroom from getting too hot. Let me just say, she's wrong. The only thing it does is make me want to take a nap. And I don't even like naps.

As I got settled at my desk, I couldn't help but notice a strange buzz circulating around the room. To the left and right of me, everyone was bent over, whispering and chattering. I tapped my desk neighbor, Logan, on the shoulder, and he turned to face me.

"What's going on?"

"New meat," he answered.

"New meat? In the cafeteria? What kind is it?"

He gave me a look and turned around.

"What'd I say?" I mumbled. I pulled out my math book and focused on the front of the classroom. That's when I saw the *new meat*.

"I'd like for you all to use your voices and help me welcome our new student. This is Marley Montgomery."

I heard snickers. I heard giggling. I heard a chair screech across the linoleum floor. I even heard a fart, which was quite unfortunate, because that meant it was close by. What I did not hear was a single "Welcome, Marley."

I stared at the newbie standing before us. She was quite possibly the coolest fifth grader I'd ever seen, and that's saying a lot, because I do have a mirror. She had long, wavy black hair and smooth, dark brown skin. She rocked tall black combat boots with a purple baby doll dress. Layers of silver necklaces dangled from her neck. She could have stepped out of a fashion magazine.

We were going to be best friends. She just didn't know it yet.

Mrs. Wood guided her to a seat near the front, and my mind pondered this sudden interest in a new friend. Kevin was my best friend. Kevin had always been my best friend. Why did I feel the need to have another? I pushed the nagging question to the back of my mind and did something I don't do very often: I paid attention to the math lesson.

When the bell rang for lunch, I hurried to where Marley stood rifling through her backpack. I decided to nudge her a little so she would notice me, but at the same time, one of my classmates, a short kid named Bobby, knocked into my arm. I smacked Marley in the ear and her head bounced around like one of those bobblehead toys.

"Hey! Watch where you're going," she said. "Do you not see me?"

She didn't wait for an answer before walking away, which was probably a good thing. I sighed and followed the crowd into the lunchroom. Kevin waved me over to our usual spot. I played Dodge the Lunch Trays as I weaved and bobbed like a pro.

"I heard your class got a new student," he said with a mouthful of applesauce.

"I heard that when you talk with food in your mouth, it lets brain cells escape." He shut his mouth. "Too late."

I was busy taking out my lunch and didn't notice Marley until she bumped into me when she sat down.

"Now we're even." She smiled. "Mind if I sit here?"

I shrugged like I didn't care, but my insides were jumping for joy. "Sure."

"Who's this cool guy?" she asked, gesturing toward Kevin. I looked around like I was confused.

"A cool *guy*? There's no one here that fits that description," I joked.

Marley laughed, but Kevin looked annoyed.

"Ha ha." Kevin shot me a piercing glance. "I'm Kevin. And I *am* totally cool. Thanks for noticing."

"Hi, Kevin. I'm Marley. And you're Beulah, right?"

It was a good thing Kevin had just swallowed his mouthful of applesauce, because otherwise his burst of laughter would have sprayed it all over us.

"Actually, I go by Blue."

She nodded. "Yeah, if my name was Beulah, I'd go by Blue, too. Or Red. Or Yellow. Even Turquoise would be better than Beulah."

Kevin said, "I think I'm going to start calling you Turquoise."

When I said what I was going to start calling him, he changed his mind about the Turquoise thing.

"Where are you from?" I asked Marley. Before she had a chance to respond, Shane Butts came up to our table.

"Hey, Blue."

"Hey, Shane." I looked down. Not because I was shy, but because I happened to have a sudden interest in my apple slices.

"Are you going to the football game on Friday night?"

"Oh. I . . . uh . . . I can't."

Marley linked her arm with mine. "Are you playing?"

"Shane is the quarterback," Kevin mumbled.

"Well, see you later, Blue," Shane said. He ran his hands through his hair before he left our table and made his way to the other side of the cafeteria.

"He is so cute," Marley giggled. I just smiled.

"If I had his last name, I would never live it down," Kevin said. "But for some reason everyone thinks Shane is so cool that he never gets teased for it. It's not fair."

"What is his last name?"

I sighed. "Butts."

"Huh?"

"His name is Shane Butts," I told her, trying not to smile. The look on her face pretty much made that impossible.

"You're not joking, are you?"

"With a name like Beulah, that's not something I'd ever joke about."

Kevin snorted. "If you got married, you'd be Beulah Butts!" I threw my string cheese at him.

"Or Blue Butts," Marley chimed in. We all laughed.

"Like I'd ever marry Shane Butts anyway. *Ew.*"

"Well, if you change your mind, maybe keep your last name." Marley winked.

I shrugged and started eating my sandwich. I didn't even know if he had a girlfriend. I knew he went out with Sarah Butterfield, but she broke up with him because Anthony Chevski gave her a bigger Valentine card, and then he went out with Jenny Avila, but they broke up when her brother knocked over his bike, and then before that it was Charlotte Kennedy.

I think. I mean, I hardly pay attention to those kinds of things.

I changed the subject, and we finished the rest of our lunch without any more Shane talk. The afternoon flew by until it was time to walk home.

Marley found me in my usual spot under a tree. I was waiting for my slowpoke brother Jackson.

"Where's Kevin?" Marley asked. "Is he mad about Shane?"

"Shane? Why would he be mad about Shane?" The thought was so absurd it made me giggle.

Jackson walked up, being nosy, as usual. "Shane Butts? The most popular guy in school? What about him?"

"Mind your own business," I said at the same time Marley said, "He's your sister's crush." I tried to elbow her, but it was too late.

Jackson howled like a wolf singing to the moon.

"You like Butts?" He stopped his squealing and started to dance. "You like Butts! Blue likes Butts!"

"I do not!" I tried to tell him, but it didn't matter. I grabbed Marley's arm and pulled her down the sidewalk.

"Sorry," she said quietly.

"BLUE LIKES BUTTS."

"It's okay. He's always like this. If we're going to be friends, let's get one thing clear: Never, ever, *ever* talk to my brother. Don't even look him in the eye. Okay?"

"BLUE LIKES BUTTS."

"Right. Got it." She glanced quickly back at Jackson, but I watched her. She did not look him in the eye.

"BLUE LIKES BUTTS."

I turned around. "No, I don't, 'cause I don't like you and you're the biggest butt of all."

Jackson made a pretend sad face and then pointed right in my face. "Blue likes *b-u-t-t-s*!"

I was going to kick him in his *b-u-t-t-s* in about two seconds if he didn't shut his mouth.

"So what did you think of your first day of school?" I asked Marley.

"BLUE LIKES BUTTS."

"It was good. Mrs. Wood is nice," Marley answered.

"BLUE LIKES BUTTS."

"But why is her classroom so dark?"

"It's because she thinks—"

Jackson tapped me on the shoulder. "Hey, Blue. I heard you like Butts."

Marley dropped her backpack on the ground. "That's it. My mama taught me not to hit a boy, but if you say that one more time, it's on."

Jackson stopped in his tracks. "Wh-what?"

"You heard me," she said, stepping closer to my evil brother. "I will make you wish you were never born."

I watched Jackson's face change as each thought passed through his tiny little pea brain. He finally shrugged.

"Okay." He tightened the straps on his backpack and pulled up the waist of his jeans before stretching out his legs. He had a look in his eye, like some sort of terrible plan was all coming together. He walked right up to Marley, put his hand on her shoulder, and let out a deep breath. "Your friend, my sister, LOVES HER SOME BIG OLE BUTTS!" Then, without a moment's hesitation, he took off running down the sidewalk before Marley could grab him.

"It's okay," I said as Marley picked up her backpack. "Thanks for trying."

"Oh, I'm not done. I'm just giving him a head start. I run track."

"Are you really going to beat him up?"

"Of course not. But he doesn't know that." Then she pushed her backpack into my arms and took off down the street after Jackson.

I was right. She really was the coolest fifth grader I'd ever seen.

12

I desperately needed money, and I decided Spring Break was the perfect time to make some.

I'd found the most beautiful pair of shoes, and I really needed them for when I met London Malloy. She would be so impressed by these beautiful works of art. They were extra-special because they reminded me of my mom's fingernails—red and sparkly. They looked like Dorothy's shoes in *The Wizard of Oz*, my mom's most favorite movie. When I looked at them, I practically heard munchkins singing.

Like I said, I *really* needed those shoes.

One of the drawbacks of living in a house full of males is that they do not share my opinion on the importance of shoes. Still, I grabbed the photo of the shoes, which I'd printed at school, and went to find my father, determination boiling inside of me.

"Hey, Dad. Can I talk to you about something? It's really important."

He took off his reading glasses and put his book on the table next to him. "What is it, Blue?"

I thrust my picture at him and pointed to the shoes of utter perfection.

"I really need these shoes, which means I need you to get me these shoes." He immediately put his glasses back on and reached for his book. "Wait, Dad. What are you doing?"

"Didn't I just buy you a pair of shoes?"

"No."

He gave me a look.

"Well, that was, like, two months ago."

"It was, like, eleven days ago."

"But I neeeed these ones! I want to wear them when we go to LA and meet London Malloy!"

Just then Jackson burst into the room, with Arnie hot on his heels. "Dad! Dad! You totally need to get us this game." He thrust a picture at Dad. "It's the new *Four Force Seven*. Come on, Dad!"

"Come on, Dad!" Arnie repeated.

"I seem to recall you already getting two new video games for your birthday."

"Yeah, but *Four Force Seven* wasn't out yet. I neeeed it," he whined. What a baby.

"Um, I believe our father already told you no," I said. "Besides, he's buying me shoes, so he won't have any money for your lame game."

Dad opened his book. That was not a good sign.

"No, Blue. I'm sorry, Jackson. If you want to buy these things, then you'll both have to buy them yourselves. You have money saved up."

"But not enough," Jackson said.

"I only have fifteen dollars. The shoes are thirty dollars."

"Then I guess you'll have to find ways to earn some more money."

He started reading his book, and I knew there was no use in trying to talk him into it. I slumped away, utterly defeated. I needed those shoes.

"Hey," Jackson said, coming up behind me. "I have an idea. Arnie and I have fifteen dollars and thirty-six cents. Well, actually I have fifteen dollars and Arnie has thirty-six cents, but anyway, what if you loan us your money? Then we'll have enough money to get our game. Right, Arnie?"

"Right, Arnie," Arnie repeated.

"No way, Jackson. Here's a thought: Why don't you lend me your money and I'll have enough for my shoes? Sound good?" I turned away without waiting for an answer. "Nice try, though."

"Wait a minute," Jackson said. I stopped but I didn't turn

around. "What if we come up with some kind of contest? Whoever wins gets the other person's fifteen dollars."

I thought about it. "Maybe. What kind of contest?"

"Let's play *Four Force Six* and whoever wins—"

"Not gonna happen. I'm not playing against you on your favorite game ever. What about a jump-rope contest?"

"Yeah right, Blue. Weren't you the third-grade champion?"

"Was I? I can't remember."

Seth came around the corner just then. "What are you two arguing about now?"

We both tried to explain at the same time, and eventually he held up his hand. "Okay. I've heard enough. There's an easy solution to this. Why don't you see who can earn the most money? Start right now for the rest of today and the winner takes it all."

That was too risky. What if I lost?

"Unless you're both scared . . ."

Um, scared? "Fine," I said. "Jackson, are you in?"

He gulped. "Okay. Whoever makes the most money gets to keep all the money, including the fifteen dollars we each already have." He held out his hand, and I shook it.

"Time starts now," Seth said, walking away. Jackson and I stared at each other for a split second before running in opposite directions.

"Come on, Arnie. Let's go," Jackson called while I went back to my room.

I rifled through my things, desperate for inspiration. I needed to make money, but how? I paced around for a few minutes, sweat dripping down my back, until Seth showed up in my doorway.

"You have no idea what to do, do you?"

"I got nothin'."

"Last summer I made fifty dollars a day doing yard work."

"Well, it's not summer, Seth."

"No, but it's springtime now. People are starting to plant flowers and water their plants and mow their lawns. . . ."

"Ew, Seth. I don't want to push a heavy lawn mower."

"Then I guess you don't want those shoes. Have fun watching Jackson play his video game." Seth shrugged and left.

I thought about it some more. I mean, it's not like I had any better ideas, and I was wasting precious time. I finally sat down at my desk and started drawing out a flier. I listed the different services I could provide, such as raking leaves, mowing lawns, trimming bushes, picking up trash, and watering grass and flowers. I made prices for each task and decorated the flier's edges with pretty flowers.

Skipping down the hallway, I could already imagine

the sparkling red magic all over my feet. Those shoes were mine.

I quickly printed out twenty fliers on the copier in my dad's office and rushed out the door. I went from house to house and passed them out. Most people weren't home, so I left a flier on their door. The people who were home just smiled politely, said "No thank you," and shut the door. Feeling defeated, I headed home.

As I got closer to Jane's house, I noticed she was sitting on her front porch. I put my head down and tried not to look at her as I passed by.

"What have you got there?" she called out. I ignored her and kept walking. "Blue? What have you been passing out all over the neighborhood?"

I sighed and waited as she approached me. I handed her my last flier. Her lips moved while she read my list.

"I see. So you're going around the neighborhood looking to do yard work?" She threw her head back and laughed. "I don't suppose you see the irony in this?"

"Huh?"

She looked down at the flier again. "I'll tell you what. You can do everything on this list for me. I want you to mow the lawn and trim my raspberry bush. I also want you to clear out my flower beds and pull the weeds. But here's the catch, Blue Warren. You're going to do it all for free."

"What?" I think I actually squeaked.

"That's right. You owe me, as I remember." She put her pink-manicured hand on my shoulder. I was surprised her nails weren't black. *Like her soul.*

"Hurry along. And do a good job. I have some errands to run this afternoon, but I'll be around for a little while."

I stomped toward my house, my blood boiling. How did this even happen? I'd purposely skipped her house so I wouldn't have to talk to her, and now I was stuck doing all her yard work for free! Of course, I could say no, but would she march right over and tell my dad what we did with the newspapers in her backyard? It wasn't worth the risk.

I rolled our lawn mower toward her haunted house, so angry I could hardly see straight. That's when I noticed my brothers.

They were carrying a brown paper bag and going door-to-door. I couldn't see what they were doing, and they stayed away from me. It didn't matter anyway; I was wasting all my precious time working for free. Even if they somehow figured out a way to earn one dollar, they were going to win.

I glanced at Jane the Witch, sitting so smug on her front porch. She watched me as I started down one side of the stupid grass, pushing the stupid lawn mower along. After I finished, I walked the stupid mower back into the garage and grabbed our stupid hedge clippers. I started trimming the stupid raspberry bush and then I started eating her stupid delicious raspberries.

The sun beat down, making my whole body break out in a sweat. Great. Now I was sticky *and* penniless.

It felt like hours passed as I made my way over to start on her stupid flowers. I unraveled her hose so I could water them, but she stopped me.

"Here, use this." She handed me a watering can and a cold glass of what looked like lemonade. Or poison.

I hesitated before taking the glass. It was so hot, and I was so thirsty. I licked my lips, and before I could stop myself, I put the glass up to my mouth and poured the sweet, icy liquid down my incredibly parched throat as fast as I could.

Jane laughed. "I'll get you some more while you start on those flowers."

I nodded, grateful for the lemonade but still upset that I was spending my whole day working for free. My beautiful Dorothy shoes were forever gone. I sighed as I filled up the watering can. I was about to start when she came back out with the second glass.

"Thanks." I took a few swigs, not sure what else to say.

"Have a seat, Blue. Take a break for a minute."

I would have rather kept working, but I didn't say this.

I sat down on the concrete steps and fidgeted with the hem of my shorts.

"Not exactly how you pictured spending your day, is it?" I didn't respond. "So why are you trying to earn money? That is what you're doing, isn't it? Trying to earn some money?"

I just shrugged, but she kept waiting for me to say something. "I wanted a new pair of shoes." I kind of huffed my answer.

"Want*ed*? You don't want them anymore?"

"No, I still want them. It's just . . . never mind."

"You can talk to me, you know. Are these shoes special?" she asked, but I shrugged my answer again. I didn't know how to explain to her how important the shoes were to me. That it would be like having a piece of my mother with me when I met London Malloy.

We sat in silence for a few moments, me sipping the lemonade and Jane staring into the distance, no doubt thinking about some potion or spell.

"Well, what do these shoes look like?" she finally asked.

"They're red and sparkly and perfect. I saw them in the JCPenney catalogue and they go up to a size seven. I'm a size six, but, whatever, it's not like I need them." What just happened? Jane wasn't my friend. I couldn't believe I'd just told her all of that.

And also, I lied. I absolutely *did* need those shoes.

"I see," Jane said. "Did you want these shoes for something specific?"

"No. Well, sort of. It's hard to explain."

"So try," she said, nudging me softly with her shoulder.

I didn't know what to say, but she continued to stare at me—so much so that I finally said, "The shoes remind me of someone very important. Someone I'm trying very hard not to forget."

Jane nodded like she understood, but she couldn't possibly. "You know, most people are sad when they remember people from their past, but I think the real tragedy is when you forget them." She looked down at her watch. "Speaking of which, I almost forgot that I have some errands to run. I'll be back in a bit. Please don't forget to clear out the flower beds; I just picked up some daisy and sunflower seeds I want to get planted this weekend. And you know what else? Why don't you pull the weeds that are growing along the side of the house, too? That should keep you pretty busy." She turned to leave but then added, "Sorry about your shoes. I understand how you feel. At least there's always tomorrow."

She clearly didn't understand anything at all. I wasn't talking about just the shoes. I tried not to groan out loud as I picked up the trowel and headed toward the planters that lined her windows. I'd already pulled the weeds and watered one when Jane's garage door opened and she drove away. Good riddance.

It was still so hot, and I finished the rest of the lemonade in no time. I wished I had more. Trying not to think about it, I worked as fast as I could, cleaning and watering all her flower beds and planters. As I carried the trash bag to the side of the house where Jane kept the trash cans, I saw my brothers working their way around the neighborhood again. What were they up to?

I was halfway through with the weeds on the side of the house when Jane pulled into the driveway and parked in her garage. A few minutes later, she came out and inspected my work right in front of me. She put a finger in the stupid flower garden to check the moisture of the soil. She went into the stupid backyard and searched for a lone leaf that I might've missed. She marched back and forth, making sure the stupid raspberry bush was perfect. I wanted to stomp all over her delicious raspberries.

I wiped the sweat off my forehead with a filthy hand while I waited. I knew I looked disgusting, but I didn't care. I was so ready to leave.

"I think you've done enough for today. Thank you for your help, Blue."

I mumbled a "You're welcome." Picking up the tools I'd

brought over, I walked away without so much as a backward glance or even a goodbye.

I dragged myself up the stairs and started a shower. I closed my eyes and let the cool water wash the hard day's work off me. What a stupid, stupid day. Stupid contest. Stupid yard work. Stupid red sparkle shoes.

No. The red sparkle shoes weren't stupid. They were bedazzled perfection.

After I was all dressed, I went downstairs to look for Jackson and Arnie. They were sitting on the couch, watching cartoons and eating popsicles. Jackson barely looked up.

"How much did she pay you?" Jackson asked.

"A lot," I answered. I wasn't quite ready to admit my defeat just yet. "What did you and Arnie do? How much money did you make?"

"Ten cents." Arnie smiled with purple drool from the popsicle.

"Not cents, Arnie. I keep telling you. It's ten dollars."

"Ten dollars," Arnie said.

"What? How did you earn that much money? You didn't even do anything." It was so unfair.

Jackson turned down the television and sat up straight. "We worked very hard today, didn't we, Arnie?" Arnie nodded very seriously. "We sold flower bouquets to all of our neighbors."

"Flower bouquets? How? We don't have any flowers."

"We picked them," Arnie said.

"What do you mean, you picked them? Where did you pick them from?"

"We walked around the neighborhood and picked them out of our neighbors' yards," Jackson said. "They had so many pretty ones to choose from."

"Red and yellow and blue, like you," Arnie said.

I just stood there. I couldn't speak.

"What?" Jackson asked.

"You . . . you . . ." I took a deep breath. "You mean to tell me, you picked the neighbors' flowers and then *sold them back to them? Their own flowers?*"

"For ten cents!" Arnie said proudly.

"Ten *dollars.*" Jackson shook his head.

I turned around and stormed out of the room. I marched upstairs and pulled all the money out of my piggy bank. Fifteen one-dollar bills, all crumpled up, fell into a pile on my bed. I scooped them up, stomped back into the living room and dumped them all in Jackson's lap.

"What are you doing?"

"You won," I told him. "Jane didn't pay me anything. I had to do it for free because we trashed her yard. Enjoy your game."

I left him there and went to my room. My back muscles

were sore from all the digging. I stretched out on my bed like a cat. Which reminded me of a lion. Which reminded me of the Cowardly Lion. Which reminded me of the shoes. A few minutes later, there was a knock on my door.

"Go away," I said, rolling over.

Jackson opened the door and sat on my bed. "Here," he said, giving me back my crumpled dollars. "Just keep it. I messed up the yard, too. It's not fair."

Who was this kid lately? The Jackson I knew wouldn't have cared. He would be halfway to the store by now, singing the theme song to *Four Force Seven*. If it even had a theme song.

"Besides, with the ten dollars we earned, I only need five more dollars and then I can buy the game anyway." He stood up to leave.

"Wait." I counted out five dollars and held it out to him. "Here. At least one of us will get what we want."

"Really?" He jumped up and down. "Thank you, thank you, thank you!" Maybe it was the heat of the day, or maybe it was just pure exhaustion, but when he tried to hug me, I actually let him. It felt weird, like a wiggly octopus trying to use its tentacles for the first time. I managed a smile as he ran out of the room, waving the money in his hand. "Dad, will you take me to the store?" he called out.

A few minutes later they left, but I stayed in bed. I think

I dozed off, because the next thing I knew, the doorbell was ringing.

"Is anybody here?" I called. No answer. The doorbell rang again. I pulled my tired legs off the bed and dragged myself to the front door. When I swung it open, no one was there. I almost cried. All that work getting out of bed was for nothing? I was about to close the door when I saw it.

There on the welcome mat was a small box. I bent down to open it and gasped. One exquisite pair of the most beautiful red sparkle shoes you could ever imagine was staring up at me. The jewels on the shoes caught the sunlight just right, and they looked even more magical than I'd ever thought possible. I lifted up the box, and a small piece of paper fell out. I picked it up.

Our memories make us who we are.

Love,
J

I searched the space between our house and Jane's, but she was already gone. I stood in place, not sure what to do. My eyes stung with the beginning of tears. Then I cradled my shoes in my arms and quietly shut the door.

13

I had to spy Arnie out of the corner of my eye a few times before it finally registered that he was up to something. He was being so quiet that I almost didn't notice what he was doing. What I *should* have noticed was the fact that he was actually being quiet. I took a bite of my toast and chewed slowly, squinting my eyes as I waited for him to make another move. It didn't take long.

Arnie's entire diet consisted of three food groups: the hot dogs, the yogurts, and the cheeses. I don't know how, but he survived entirely off of those three items alone. And the occasional cookie, of course. This morning, he was eating cut-up fried hot dogs with a side of strawberry yogurt.

How original.

Only, as I began to watch him, I realized the little weirdo was only eating half of his pile of hot dogs. The other slices were being methodically placed into the pocket of his pants. Why in the world would Arnie want a pocket full of mushed-up hot dogs? So gross.

I was determined to find out what he was up to. I slurped down the last of my chocolate milk while I waited for Arnie to finish eating. He was taking foreverrrrr. I thought about all the reasons he could be collecting pieces of hot dog.

Maybe he thought if he planted them in the garden, little dogs would grow.

Maybe he was tired of his rock collection and was moving on to something more original.

Maybe he had a hungry imaginary friend.

Maybe he was saving them for a midnight snack.

Arnie finally finished his last spoonful of yogurt and swung down from his chair. I casually pretended to yawn and stood up, too. When he left the room, I followed to see where he went. He headed straight for his bedroom.

I waited another minute and then crept up the stairs, stepping around the left side of the third stair, because that one creaked. I tiptoed down the hall until I was in front of Arnie's bedroom, and then I put my ear up to the door to listen. The only noise coming from inside his room was a quiet scraping sound. Whatever he was doing, it couldn't be that exciting. I had just decided to leave him in peace when the door flew open in my face. He looked just as surprised to see me as I was to see him. Then again, he was wearing nothing but his underwear and a cowboy hat. I was fully clothed, of course, because I am a civilized human being.

"Whatcha doing?" Arnie asked me.

"Huh? What?" I looked at a framed picture hanging on the wall and pretended to wipe some dust off the glass.

"Whatcha doing?"

I tried to deflect. "What are *you* doing, Arnie? Hmmm?"

He looked over his shoulder. "Nothing."

"Well, I'm doing nothing, too."

We eyed each other, and I can only imagine I looked at him as suspiciously as he looked at me. I tried not to look away first, on account of the dog rule. With dogs, WHOEVER LOOKS AWAY FIRST IS THE LOSER. In this house, I try never to lose. I leaned against the door frame and raised my eyebrows. Arnie tried to push me out of the way and close his door. He must've been doing something good in there if he didn't want me to see it.

I was totally going to see it.

"Well, I'm going to go now," I told him casually, swinging one leg forward and back.

"Arnie's going, too."

We stood there awkwardly, so I finally turned around to leave. He waited for me to close my bedroom door before he moved. I know this because I heard his footsteps and saw his shadow pass under my door.

I left my room and slithered back down the hall like a snake. I kind of felt like a snake, too, spying on my little brother. But it was up to me to protect our family and to protect our home.

Not really. I just wanted to know what he was doing with the hot dogs.

I slid through a crack in his door and quickly scanned the room for any obvious oddities, but it looked just like his usual messy room. It did have a rotten-egg smell, but, sadly, I was pretty sure that was normal. I needed to search his room for anything suspicious, so I started with his bed. I shook out all of his blankets, and when I did, something black fell to the floor. I dropped the blankets back onto the bed and bent down to investigate. A fuzzy black caterpillar was just starting to uncurl itself.

I picked it up and let it crawl on my hand, petting its soft, prickly fur with my finger. So this is what Arnie was trying to hide. He had a pet caterpillar! And he was probably trying to feed it the hot dogs. Children can be so adorable sometimes.

The caterpillar had crawled across my hand, so I put up my other hand for it to keep going. I hoped Arnie hadn't named him yet, because he really looked like a Herman.

"Hi, little guy. Is your name Herman?" It curled itself back up, but not because it didn't like the name Herman. It was probably just scared of my voice, that's all.

The door swung open, and Arnie stood in the doorway, a toy gun holster now strapped around his waist. It took the already inappropriate outfit to a whole 'nother level. Why, for the love of ice cream, did the boys in my family insist on walking around in just their underwear all the time?

"This is Arnie's room. Get out."

"I was only looking for you. Besides, I found your little secret." Arnie glanced back at his bed. "He's so cute. I understand why you wanted to keep him, but we need to take him back outside."

"Why? Arnie wants him to be a pet."

"Okay, but you need to keep him *outside*," I told him. "He doesn't belong in a house."

"Arnie likes his home."

I shook my head. "If he sleeps with you, he might get hurt. What if you roll over on him?"

Arnie looked confused. "He won't get hurt. He has a shell."

"No, Arnie, that's not a shell. That's just fur."

"Fur?" Arnie laughed, clutching his stomach and doubling over. I waited with my hand on my hip for him to finish. Herman was sitting in the palm of my other hand. "That's not fur. Fruit Ninja doesn't have fur!"

Fruit Ninja? Geez, with a name like that, he might as well have named the poor thing Beulah.

"I think he likes the name Herman better," I said.

"No Herman!"

"Okay, okay. I was just trying to help." I cupped the caterpillar in my hand. "Let's take him outside and let him have some fresh air."

"He doesn't go outside. He doesn't like it," Arnie said.

"Of course he likes it. He's an animal."

"It's too cold."

"What? It's not too cold. It's the middle of Spring, silly."

Arnie shook his head and started to back away from me.

"We're taking him outside," I demanded. "*Now*, Arnie."

He sighed and stopped backing up. When he came toward me, I thought it was to take the caterpillar out of my hand. Instead, he got on his knees and pulled out a box from underneath his bed.

"What's that for?" I asked.

"It's his house." Arnie looked confused again.

"Arnie, that box is huge. You put that tiny thing in there?" No wonder the bug was still alive. He'd been living in a mansion with all the hot dogs a caterpillar could want.

Arnie stood up, the box in his hands. "Arnie's ready!"

"We don't have to carry the whole box down. We can just hold him."

"But Dad will see Fruit Ninja."

"I told you, Dad isn't going to care. Besides, he's so small he won't even notice him in my hand."

"You held Fruit Ninja?" Arnie peered down at my hand, confused. "Where?"

I looked at Arnie strangely. "I'm holding him right now."

"No. Arnie's holding him."

"No, I'm holding him. Look. He's crawling on my hand."

Arnie stared blankly down at my hands. Then he took the giant box to the bed and lifted the lid. "No. Nope. I told you. Arnie's holding him."

I followed him over to the bed and peered into the box. There, tucked into the corner, wedged between two rocks, was a tiny box turtle. He had a yellow stripe down the center of his shell, with bright yellow fireworks on either side.

"Arnie! What is that?"

"Fruit Ninja."

I thrust the caterpillar into his face. "I thought *this* was Fruit Ninja."

Arnie smiled. "That's Fruit Ninja's food. Arnie lost him." He reached out to take the caterpillar out of my hand, but I snatched it back.

"This is *not* Fruit Ninja's food. This is now Herman, *thank you very much!*"

"Oh. Well, can we take Fruit Ninja outside now?"

"Are you crazy? Dad's never going to let you keep a turtle. You have to let him go."

"You said Dad would let Arnie keep him!"

"No, I said Dad would let you keep a *caterpillar*. Where did you get a turtle, anyway?"

Arnie shuffled his feet and looked away. "Mrs. Atchinson's garden."

"Arnie! You know you're not allowed in her garden, not since you stole all her sugar snap peas that one time."

"Arnie had to catch Fruit Ninja."

"Arnie did *not* have to catch Fruit Ninja." I thought back to earlier in the week. "Did you sneak away on Tuesday when we had that picnic?" He nodded and stared at the ground shyly. "Arnie! That was four days ago!" I finally remembered the whole reason I'd been following him in the first place. "Wait a minute. Have you been feeding him hot dogs?"

Arnie nodded. "And yo-yurt and cheese."

I looked into the box at Fruit Ninja. "Does he eat all of that?"

Arnie shook his head. "Fruit Ninja isn't very hungry."

"Of course he's hungry. What did you say his name was again . . . ?"

"Fruit Ninja," Arnie said, sounding annoyed.

"Right. And it still didn't occur to you to try feeding him, you know, *fruit*?"

Arnie looked surprised. "Arnie did feed him fruit."

"Good." I sighed with relief. "Because you have to feed him what *he* likes, not what *you* like."

"He eats raspberries! Arnie fed him all of Arnie's raspberries!" He looked down at his turtle and his chin started to tremble. "Arnie's bad?"

"No, Arnie's not bad—I mean, *you're* not bad. But we have to let him go. It's not okay to take a wild animal out of its environment, Arnie. He needs to find proper food and be with his family."

"Arnie is his family."

I sighed. How could I make him understand? "Fruit Ninja has a turtle mommy and a turtle daddy outside somewhere. He might even be lucky enough to have an amazing and perfect turtle sister, just like you do. So we should put him back, don't you think?"

Arnie vigorously shook his head. "Nope."

"Arnie, we're taking the turtle outside where he belongs."

"No!"

"Then I'm telling Dad."

"Noooo!"

"Well, then help me carry him outside, and let's find a spot for him."

"Find a spot for who?" Jackson asked, barging into Arnie's room.

"Go away," I said at the same time Arnie said, "Fruit Ninja."

Jackson walked right up to the bed and looked inside the box. "Whoa. You got a turtle?"

"He's Arnie's turtle," Arnie said. "Not Blue's turtle." He reached inside the box and picked up Fruit Ninja, cradling him in his arms.

"He's no one's turtle because he's a wild animal. I'm trying to explain to Arnie that he can't keep him," I said.

"Blue's right, you can't keep him . . ." Jackson started, then finished, ". . . on your own. But with our help, you can."

Arnie held tight to Fruit Ninja as he jumped up and down, grinning ear to ear.

"What? No, Jackson!" I sputtered, but it was too late. Jackson was already carrying the box out of the room, and Arnie was following. "If Dad sees—"

"He won't, he's next door talking to Jane."

"Why is he talking to her?" I asked. That seemed odd. I really hoped they weren't going to become friends.

Jackson shrugged. "I don't know. Who cares? We have a turtle!"

"*Arnie* has turtle," Arnie said.

I followed my brothers down the stairs, with Jackson carrying the box, Arnie carrying Fruit Ninja, and me carrying Herman. I stopped to google what turtles eat, and then I went to the fridge and collected everything we had available: one banana, two carrots, three strawberries, and a handful of lettuce. I also filled a dish with water before I went outside to meet up with my brothers.

By the time I got there, they'd already found a pretty good spot to make his home. A small flower bed surrounded the orange tree in the far corner of our yard, and Jackson was already halfway finished building an enclosure around it. He'd taken a pile of large rocks from the side of the house and carried them over to the tree to build a stone wall. I put Herman and the food on the ground and helped Jackson carry the rest of the rocks. When we finished, I stood back and admired our work.

"Not bad."

The inside of the wall had lots to offer the sweet little turtle. There were tree roots sticking out of the grass, which gave Fruit Ninja lots of little nooks and sleeping spots. He had flowers and dirt and grass, and he'd even have oranges when they dropped to the ground. Normally the orange tree was a pain. We always had to clean it up, and we never ate as many oranges as it dropped. But this was perfect for Fruit Ninja. Jackson had placed a couple of rocks inside the wall along with the dish of water I'd brought outside. I piled all the food next to the water and hoped he would want to eat at least one of the choices.

"Okay, put the turtle in," Jackson said, bouncing with excitement, until he saw Arnie's face. "Arnie . . ."

I looked over at my youngest brother. Arnie's chin was trembling, and he was holding Fruit Ninja tightly as he backed away from us.

"Arnie," I told him, "it's okay. Jackson made him an awesome home. He's going to be so happy here. Let's just see if he likes it." I put my arm around Arnie and ushered him closer to the enclosure. "Put him down near the food," I added, cringing at the thought of all those hot dogs. At least he had some berries to hold him over.

Poor Fruit Ninja.

Arnie reluctantly placed him in the grass. The turtle went straight for the bananas and started eating.

Poor, poor Fruit Ninja.

"Arnie? Next time you decide to keep an animal and give it a name, pay better attention to what you choose. Did you name him Hot Dog Ninja?"

"No." Arnie laughed. "Silly Blue! Why would Arnie name him that?"

"That's a good question. Kind of like how 'Why would you try to feed him hot dogs?' is a good question."

Arnie's laugh died down, and he looked at the turtle eating the fruit. "Oh."

Jackson shook his head, and I gave Arnie a hug. "I don't

think Dad will even notice him back here. Let's just make sure he always has food and water, okay?" The boys nodded. I crouched down and took both of Arnie's hands into my own. "Arnie? No more hiding secret pets in your room, got it? It's not good for them."

Arnie looked confused. "Can I hide one if not in Arnie's room?"

"No. Don't hide them at all."

"Can I hide them in your room?"

"Definitely not."

"What if they were in Arnie's room but now they aren't?" he asked.

"What do you mean?"

Arnie looked at the ground. "Arnie had a pet snake, but he went away." Even Jackson looked nervous when he heard that.

"Arnie! If you find an animal, you have to take care of it properly!" I let go of his hands as I felt my body go cold as ice. "Where did the snake go?"

"I dunno. He ran away from Arnie's room." Arnie held out his arms and pretended to be an airplane as he flew toward the house. "Now he's freeee!"

Oh, no.

14

It was a beautiful sunny day, we only had a month left of school, and it was the weekend. Life was grand. Kevin and I lay on our backs in my front yard, stretched out over the green grass and scattered dandelions.

"Did you ever finish your mom's favorite book?" Kevin asked.

That perked me right up. "You mean *Charlotte's Web*?" I nodded, excited to share more. "It was so good, Kevin! The ending was so sad when—"

Just then, a water balloon exploded near my shoulder, and the burst of water hit me on the side of my face and in my ear. I jumped up, but not before Kevin got blasted on his knee. His water splash made it look like he peed all over himself.

Kevin flew up and we scanned our surroundings, but I

couldn't find anyone around us. I turned just in time to get pelted on my back. Where were they?

"Hey," I yelled, spinning in place. There was still no one to be found. Where were they coming from? Less than a minute later, I had my answer.

One after another, water balloons exploded all around us. By the tenth balloon, I finally realized where they were coming from. Somebody wasn't hiding around the corner and throwing them at us—they were *dropping* them on us. I looked up. Seth and his friends were on top of the roof.

Seth laughed at the same time I turned my face right into a bright blue water balloon. The smacking sound it made caused everyone to freeze on the spot.

"Blue? Are you okay?" Seth called down.

I would have told him no if I could speak. The pain from my nose was pulsing across my entire face. I cupped my hands over my nose, and when I pulled them away, there was blood everywhere.

"Sef, you awe in sho much twouble!" I tried to say. Kevin backed away from me. He isn't so brave when it comes to blood.

Seth and his two buddies quickly climbed down from the roof. The blood from my nose was dripping onto the grass, staining the perfectly manicured green.

"You get away fwom me, Sef. I tink you bwoke my nose."

"Let me see it, Blue." Seth reached for my hands, but I smacked him away. "Don't be a baby. Let me see it." I pushed him as hard as I could, leaving two bloody handprints across the front of his shirt.

I heard the front door slam and then my father asked, "What's going on out here? Blue, what happened?"

"Your son, Sef, hit me in da face wif a water bawoon."

"He what?"

I pointed at Seth and tried again. "Sef hit me wif a water bawoon!"

"It was an accident, I didn't mean to hit her face. We were just dropping them and she—"

"Dropping them? Dropping them from where?" He looked up. "Were you on top of the roof again? How many times have I told you—"

"Dad!" Jackson came flying out of the house. "Arnie broke my Batman!" He was holding two broken pieces of superhero in his hands. "I told him not to touch it and now it's broken!"

Arnie's cries were getting louder as he made his way out the front door. Seth's friends gave him a look and started walking as fast as they could away from our house.

Arnie wobbled onto the lawn, still screaming and crying. He had a very suspicious welt on his left cheek.

"Jackson hit Arnie!" he said through tears. "Jackson's bad."

Kevin was the next to flee. I didn't blame him. I would have gone with him if I wouldn't leave a blood trail for my family to eventually find.

"Enough!" my father roared to the Warren children. "Blue, is your nose broken?"

I shook my head. "I don't fink so."

He checked my nose real good, then said, "Go get cleaned up and meet us in the car. Seth, strap Arnie into his car seat. Jackson, get into the car now and buckle up."

Two words: Road. Trip.

"No." Seth backed away. "No, Dad. Please don't do it. I'll do anything. Anything you ask. But please don't make me do this."

"You should have thought of that before you climbed up on the roof and attacked your sister. You know the rules. All electronics stay home. Put them in the house and get in the car."

I went upstairs to wash my face and change my clothes. By the time I went back outside, my family was buckled into the car and waiting in the driveway.

"Get in," my dad ordered. I got in.

My dad drives a minivan. I climbed all the way into the

back, behind Jackson and Arnie, so I had an entire row to myself. Dad backed out of the driveway.

"Why does Seth get shotgun?" I asked in what I thought was a very polite voice but what in reality might have been a tad bit whiny.

"Because he was outside when it was time to get in the van and you were not."

"But . . . but . . . I wasn't out here because he tried to kill me!"

Seth turned around. "I was not trying to kill you and you know it. I was just—"

"Silence!"

We silenced.

"Are we there yet?" Jackson asked.

"No."

My dad leaned forward and turned on the radio. Light classical music drifted through the speakers and filled the car with the peaceful sound of an orchestra. After a few minutes, I closed my eyes and let the music carry me away. I dreamt of my upcoming trip to the set of *Family Tree* and wondered for the millionth time what it would be like to meet London Malloy. I was trying to decide if we would be instant best friends or if it would happen more casually over time when—

"ARNIE TOUCHED ME!" Jackson screamed.

"No Arnie didn't," Arnie said, wide-eyed.

"Yes you did, you little Batman torturer. You touched my pinky nail right here." Jackson held up his pinky finger.

"Arnie did not touch!" Arnie screamed. "NO!"

"Actually, Dad, to be fair, I did see Arnie touch Jackson," Seth said. Arnie started his scream-cry. *Not* my favorite sound.

"No! Arnie did not touch!" he insisted though tears.

"Arnie did touch," I said. He tried to turn around and hit me, but because he was strapped into his car seat, he couldn't reach. But he did hit someone.

"Arnie hit me! Arnie hit me!" Jackson yelled. "The Batman torturer touched me *and* he hit me. You need to punish him. He's out of control!"

That's when my dad pulled over on the side of the road.

"Everyone out."

We slowly unbuckled and climbed out, everyone except Arnie. He swung his legs back and forth as he watched from his car seat through the open door.

"We are a family. We are going to sit in the car, and we are going to drive up to the mountains. We are going to sing songs and have fun and love one another the entire way, you got it?" We nodded. "Blue, you sit in the very back with Jackson. Seth, you sit next to Arnie. There will be no more fighting. The next person who picks a fight will be strapped to the top of the car, and it looks like it's going to rain. Understand?" We nodded.

As we filed back into the car, Jackson elbowed me in the ribs on purpose. I accidentally stomped on his foot. He tried to scream, but Seth clamped his hand over Jackson's mouth. The look Seth gave him was enough to keep him silent.

After a few minutes back on the road, it began to sprinkle. I stared out the window, my forehead resting on the cool glass. I watched the raindrops hit the window and slide down like one giant tear. I traced it with my finger and thought that I would LITERALLY DIE OF BOREDOM.

"Are we there yet?" Jackson asked again.

"No," my dad answered, a little more forcefully this time.

Road trips were another one of dad's creative punishments, although, if you asked me, my dad was punishing himself way more than he was punishing us.

"Where are we going?" Seth asked.

"I don't know. I thought we could go for a hike up in the mountains, but with this rain, I'm not so sure."

"Let's play a game," I said. Anything to keep me alive.

"What do you want to play?" my dad asked.

"How about A to Z?"

"Okay. What category?"

"Animals," Jackson said.

"Alligator," I shouted out.

"Bird," Jackson said.

"Cat," Seth said.

"Dog," my dad said.

"Bunny rabbits!" Arnie said.

"Arnie cheated," Jackson cried. "Arnie's a cheat and he can't play, so he's out."

"Arnie's not out!" Arnie said right before he started the scream-cry again.

"Jackson!" Seth and I said at the same time. *Ugh.*

"What'd I say?" Jackson asked over the Arnie-roars. I punched him in the leg, but it didn't count, because my dad couldn't see it.

"Let's try another game," my dad suggested. "What else can we play?"

I looked back out the window. I'd had enough of games. My head was starting to hurt, thanks to a certain tiny somebody. No one else answered him, either.

After a few minutes, Jackson asked, "Are we there yet?"

"No."

"I need my cell phone. Can I use yours?" Seth asked my dad.

"No."

"Can you change the radio station?" I asked. "I need something with a heartbeat."

"No."

"Are we there yet?" Jackson asked.

My dad pulled over again. This time it was into a small parking lot next to the base of a mountain.

"Okay, everyone out. Time to go for a walk."

"In the woods?" I asked. "In the rain?"

"It's only a light rain and there's a hiking trail. Come on, it'll be fun."

"I don't think we share the same idea of fun."

I climbed out of the van and lined up with my brothers. Tiny warm droplets landed on my still-swollen nose.

"Now what?" Seth asked, hand on his hip.

"Now we walk," my dad said. He swung Arnie onto his shoulders and started for the base of the trail. I sighed and shuffled my feet as I trekked across the parking lot after him.

We followed the path as it wound through a jungle of brush and trees. I found myself getting lost in the beauty of it all. A black-and-white bird landed on a rock as I passed and called out to me through a song. Crickets chirped and leaves rustled and our feet crunched on the rocky gravel. We talked and laughed, and for the first time that day, I enjoyed my family.

"How's your nose feeling?" Seth asked me.

I wiggled it like a bunny and it didn't hurt too bad. "It's okay," I said, "no thanks to you."

"I'm sorry, Blue. You know I would never do something like that on purpose." He sounded genuinely sorry, and he even put his arm around my shoulder for half a minute. He was so sweet, I didn't even tell him he had awful BO.

Or was that why he did it in the first place?

My dad came up from behind and put his hand firmly on Seth's shoulder. "And you're not going to do it ever again. I mean it, Seth. I don't want you on the roof anymore."

"Sorry, Dad," he mumbled. Jackson flew by us, arms outstretched and roaring like an airplane.

"Vroooom! Outta my way! I'm an airplane!" he shouted.

Arnie was doing his turkey-hop-walk ahead of us when he tripped and fell. He began to howl, "Arnie hurt toeeee!" I pulled him to his feet.

"Which toe, A-man?" I asked.

"The one that had roast beef!" He continued to cry.

Jackson turned in a wide circle and "flew" over to Arnie. I watched with a smile as he crouched down so Arnie could climb onto his back. Then they took off toward the trees, Jackson vrooming until Arnie stopped crying and began giggling hysterically.

When a gentle breeze began to pick up, I felt my hair lift

off my shoulders. "A storm's coming," Seth said.

"I think you're right," I told him, looking up at the sky.

"We should probably start heading back," my dad said.

We turned around and hiked back the way we came. I couldn't help but wonder if some of my dad's creative punishments actually worked. I would never in a million years admit that to him, but it was something to consider.

Just as we got back to the parking lot, the rain started to dump on us.

"Last one to the van is a rotten egg," my dad called. Just like that, we all took off. Even Arnie, who had demanded to walk back all by himself, raced to the van as fast as his little legs would go. I jogged slow so he wouldn't get stuck being last. It's not his fault he can't keep up.

As I got closer to the car, my heart slowed with dread. I heard Seth asking, "What do you mean you lost the keys?"

My dad was patting down his pants. "I mean I don't have them, Seth. They might've fallen out of my pocket while we were hiking."

"Or they're sitting on your seat," Jackson said, his face pressed against the window. Sure enough, there were the keys. Lightning lit up the sky, and two seconds later thunder boomed all around us. We were soaked from head to toe in an instant.

My dad pointed to a bench with a small covering. We

ran over and huddled together. It was warm rain on a warm day, and my clothes clung to my body, making me sticky and uncomfortable. I watched as my dad called Jane and asked if she would bring us our spare set of keys. As he was describing where she could find them, I wondered how often my dad spoke to Jane. I mean, since when did he even have her number?

"Jane should be here soon."

I sat down on the bench and Arnie climbed into my lap. Jackson plopped down to the right of me and Seth to the left. We had to squish together to fit on the narrow bench, and even then we barely managed to stay on.

I was wet, sticky, tired, and stuck in a thunderstorm, my head hurt, and now I was sandwiched between my smelly brother and my other, smellier brother. When Jane pulled up a while later, all full of smiles and waving out the window, I was too grouchy to wave back. My nose was starting to throb again and I just wanted to go home.

And then I got a genius idea.

"Hey, Dad, do you think I could ride home with Jane? I mean, if it's okay with her?"

"Arnie wants to ride with Jane!" he yelled.

"No, I wanna go with Jane," Jackson whined.

"It was my idea," I tried to say, but no one could hear me above their bickering.

"Arnie wants to go!"

"No, I'm going with her!"

I gave up and headed toward the van. Those two could fight it out; I'd had enough arguing with my brothers for the day.

"I've never been so popular before!" Jane held her hand up, and a warm smile spread across her face. "But I believe Blue was the first to ask, so she gets to choose." My head jerked up when she said my name. "Blue?"

"Yes, please!" I didn't even hesitate. No Arnie and no Jackson? Sign me up!

My dad and Jane exchanged a look I didn't quite understand. They seemed to know what the other was thinking without any words.

I thought about that a lot on our way home.

15

"Hold it right there, young lady."

I froze midstep, my leg still dangling in the air. I immediately started to panic, but then I stopped myself. I even chuckled. There was no way my dad knew what day it was.

"I know what day it is." He suddenly stood before me with his hand out. "Let's see it."

I sighed as I unzipped my backpack, then shoved the crumpled envelope into his hand. I held my breath as I waited. He tore open the envelope and pulled out my dreaded end of the year report card. Five and a half seconds later, he looked up.

"You have a D in science? But I thought you loved science?"

"It's not my fault," I tried to explain. "It's my teacher. She totally hates me."

My dad put his hand on my shoulder and guided me toward the kitchen. I continued to tell him all about the injustice of my grade until he opened up the fridge. I stopped, my words floating away like a fart in the wind.

It was time for a milk talk.

I resigned myself to the discussion that was to follow and slumped into a chair. I buried my head in my hands and waited for him to start. After a minute of silence, I looked up. A glass of plain milk sat before me. I took a small sip. Chocolate milk, or even strawberry milk, would've been nice, but the look on my dad's face warned me to keep that comment to myself.

By the time our glasses were empty, we had a plan to get my grade up. It started with a meeting involving both my teacher and my father. It ended with a little bit of tutoring and a lot of bit of homework over the summer.

Seth came through the kitchen door at the end, followed by Jackson. They'd heard just enough of the conversation to be pests, as usual.

"Wait a minute? Blue got a D?" Seth asked. Jackson wasn't quite as nice.

"I'm smarter than Blue! I'm smarter than Blue!" He flapped his arms like chicken wings while swinging his hips. That was a dance move that would never, ever catch on. "I'm smarter than Blue!"

"You're not smart enough to know that if you say that one more time, I will take away your video games for a week," my dad said.

I really do love that man.

"Besides," I said, "anyone can get all As in fourth grade. Fifth grade is way harder. I think we can all agree that I'm the smartest person here. Except for Dad," I added quickly. He waved as he left the room.

"We both know that's not true," Seth said with confidence. "You both don't stand a chance compared to me."

"No fair!" Jackson said. "I'm smarter than both of you, but I haven't been in fifth grade yet. You're both cheating 'cause you know I'll win."

Seth and I gave each other a look. There was no way Jackson was smarter than either of us, or even an ant, but I decided to humor him.

"Tell you what," I said. "Dad saves all our report cards. Let's compare our grades from fourth grade. Whoever got the better report card is the smartest."

"Fine," Jackson grinned. "But you're both going to be *so* sorry."

"Sure, little bro," Seth said. "Let's go."

"Go where?" Jackson asked as he followed us out of the kitchen.

"To the attic," Seth answered. "Dad keeps a box for each of us. They have all sorts of keepsake stuff, like artwork and photographs and report cards." Seth glanced at me with a wicked grin. "Prepare to be stupefied."

"You're already stupefied," I mumbled.

I had no idea what *stupefied* meant. I really, really hoped I had a good fourth-grade report card.

We climbed the narrow stairs and pulled open the door to the musty attic. Dust glittered in the air as sunbeams danced across the shadows from a tiny window.

We made our way over to the stacks of large plastic containers. Each box was labeled neatly in all-capital letters with our names across the front. Only now there was a kind-of-new one on top.

LINDA.

I glanced at Seth and saw that he was shaking. I reached out to touch him, but he jerked my hand off his shoulder.

"Is that . . . ?" Jackson asked.

"It's a box for Mom," Seth answered.

I swallowed hard. It was suddenly hard to breathe. "Should we open it?" I asked. "I want to open it."

I reached toward the box, but Seth gently pushed my hand away.

"I'll do it."

He grabbed both ends of the box and carried it over to

set under the light. He removed the lid, and all three of us peered in.

"There sure are a lot of papers," Jackson said.

"There's more than that." I pulled out a red knit scarf. "I remember Mom wearing this."

Seth nodded. "She wore it all the time." He ruffled through the papers while I wrapped the softness around my neck. I tried to breathe in her scent, but there was nothing there. Just musty attic smell.

"Let's go," Seth burst out. He was shoving a paper back into the box. "We shouldn't be up here." He tried to pull at the scarf, but I shoved him away.

"What are you talking about? Dad won't care that we looked at Mom's stuff."

"I'm serious," Seth continued. "Let's go. Now." He quickly glanced at the box before pushing us toward the door. What was he hiding? I swung around and went for the box.

"Leave it alone," he said, but I already had the lid off. I grabbed the top paper and my heart skipped a beat. It was our mother's death certificate.

"I'm okay," I told Seth. "I'm not going to break down and cry." I swallowed the lump in my throat.

Seth let out a breath and smiled. "Sorry. Give it to me and let's just go."

Jackson headed toward the doorway, but I knew

something was off. What was Seth hiding? I glanced back down at the paper, but what I read didn't make sense.

"I don't understand. Why does it say this?" I asked. Then louder, "Seth? What does this mean? *What does this mean?*" I was shaking the certificate at him, creasing it in my clenched fist.

Seth glanced at Jackson. "Put it away, Blue. Let's just go downstairs." I shook my head, but he insisted. "Come on. I'll even let you in my room."

I let him take the paper out of my hand and toss it in the box. I felt numb. He replaced the lid, then pulled me toward the exit. Jackson's voice sounded far away.

"So does this mean I'm the smartest?" he asked.

"Yeah, Jacks, you're the smartest," Seth said. "But I need to talk to Blue for a sec. Do you mind?" Jackson shrugged as I followed my oldest brother to his room and sat silently on the edge of his bed. He shut the door behind us.

"Seth, the date on that certificate is Arnie's birthday. It says Mom died on Arnie's birthday. How is that even possible?"

"Think about it, Blue. You know how it's possible."

I shook my head. "But she died in a car accident. She died the day *after* Arnie was born, on the way home from the hospital. I remember Dad sitting us down and telling us. I remember."

Seth sat next to me on the bed and put his arm around me. "He lied to us," he said quietly. "Can you think of why he would do that?"

I gulped down the pain burning in my chest and tried to speak. "Mom died giving birth to Arnie, didn't she?" I didn't need Seth to answer. The tears spilled down my cheeks. "Mom died because Arnie was born." I shrugged his arm off me and stood. "Did you know?"

"Blue, I think you should—"

"*Did you know?*" I asked him again, louder.

"No. But I've always wondered." He looked defeated. "When Dad came home with Arnie, he wouldn't look at me. You wouldn't remember, you were only seven at the time. But I was twelve, and I remember everything about that day. And Dad couldn't look me in the eyes." He lifted his head, and I could see the tears streaming down his cheeks. "I think maybe a part of me has always known."

"Why didn't you say anything?" I cried. "To Dad? To me?"

"What for?" he said, drying his face with the back of his hand. "It wasn't going to bring Mom home. And the truth is, I understand why Dad lied. Think about it, Blue. He was only trying to protect us. And Arnie."

I couldn't understand how Seth could be so calm about it all. I ran out of his room and into my own. I didn't want to stay there for another second. The room was spinning in circles as I grabbed a backpack out of my closet. I stuffed in as many clothes as I could and grabbed my favorite pillow. I couldn't stay in the house with a liar for a dad and with my littlest brother—the reason my mom was dead.

I crept out the front door and quickly crossed the street. I knocked on Kevin's door and was about to knock a second time when he finally opened the door.

"Hey." He smiled until he saw the look on my face. "What's wrong?"

"I'm running away from home, and I've decided to let you come with me," I told him.

"Uh-uh. No way, Blue. Besides, my mom is making enchiladas for dinner."

"Fine. But if anything happens to me, it'll be your fault, Kevin." I wiped a tear and turned to leave, but he stopped me.

"Wait. Are you really running away?" I nodded and Kevin sighed. "Are you going to tell me why?"

"I live with a family of killers and liars."

Kevin just stared.

"So, are you coming or what?"

"I really need to learn to tell you no. What should I pack?" I gave Kevin a quick hug.

"I don't know. Get some clothes. And food and money. And lots of candy."

He left me on the doorstep and went to grab his stuff. I ducked behind a bush and glanced toward my house, expecting someone to burst out the front door looking for me.

Nothing happened.

A few minutes later, Kevin emerged. He had on four layers of clothing and an overflowing backpack.

"Hurry. My mom just asked me to set the table." He groaned. "You better have a good reason for this, Blue Warren. You know how much I like her enchiladas."

We were halfway down the block before the guilt started to sink in. What if my dad was worried? What if Seth thought I was dead? What if Jackson cried because they couldn't find me?

Well, maybe that was taking things too far.

I told Kevin everything as we walked. I started with the stupid bet on who was the smartest and searching for our report cards. I explained how we found my mother's death certificate and what the date meant. I told him everything except the one thing I wasn't yet ready to talk about: my feelings toward Arnie and my father.

"So you're running away because your dad lied to you? I

191

get that you're upset, but it's not a reason to run away. You should talk to him."

"Did you hear anything I just told you? It's not just about my dad. It's all of it. I can't believe she was dead and I didn't even know it. When Arnie came home from the hospital, she was already gone. I'll never forgive my dad." And maybe even Arnie.

Kevin stopped. "Where should we go?"

"I don't know." I felt a fresh wave of tears sting my eyes and tried to blink them back. One escaped and slid down my cheek. "We have nowhere to go." I sat down on the sidewalk and dropped my head into my hands.

Kevin sat down next to me and put his arm around my shoulders. I leaned my head on his arm and was suddenly aware of how little planning had gone into this escape. We sat together until my head stopped spinning and I felt like I could catch my breath.

"You okay?" he asked. I nodded. Standing, we began our journey once again.

"Let's go toward the train tracks near the pond. Maybe we can find a tree to sleep under tonight." I shivered. It was going to be a long night. The sun was setting in the distance, changing the blue sky to a watercolor of orange and red. We'd been walking for over an hour.

"The train tracks? I don't know, Blue."

"Don't be a baby," I told him, crossing the street. Kevin followed, but he didn't look happy about it.

We made our way through an overgrown field, the dry grass scratching at my ankles and sticking to my shoes. The sky darkened rapidly as the sun crept lower, but we continued on.

"Where are we going?" Kevin asked, glancing behind him. I didn't have a clue, so I didn't answer.

We came out on the other side of the field just as the sun dipped below the horizon. The sudden darkness was suffocating. An owl hooted in the distance.

Back on the sidewalk, the surroundings were unfamiliar. It was a different part of town than I was used to. I heard a horn honk and jumped. I glanced behind me and saw Jane slowly pulling up next to us.

"Blue? Is that you?" she called out the window. "What are you doing so far from home? Do you need a ride somewhere?" She glanced at Kevin.

"No, I'm okay. Thanks, though." I pulled on Kevin's arm and picked up the pace. I could hear her car still coasting along next to us, but I refused to look.

"Are you sure you don't need a ride?"

I heard the car stop and her door slam shut. Jane called my name again and I turned around.

"What?" I snapped. "We don't need a ride, okay? Just

leave us alone." And then I did the worst thing I could possibly do.

I cried.

Jane walked over and held me in her arms as my body shook from the sobs. I wanted to push her away and scream and yell at her. I wanted to call her a witch and tell her that she wasn't my mother. Instead I wrapped my arms around her while she rubbed my hair. She smelled like gardenias. Not as good as honeysuckle, but close enough.

When I was finished, I wiped my wet face on my T-shirt. It was a whole lotta snot.

I watched her take a long look at our backpacks and Kevin's ridiculous layers and layers of clothing. She raised her eyebrows but said nothing. This was getting awkward.

"Well, thanks for the cry-fest. We'll just be going now." I reached for the backpack I'd dropped in my moment of self-pity, but Jane got to it first.

"I can give you a ride. Where are you headed?" She was already walking back to her car, my hijacked backpack secured tightly in her arms.

"That's okay, we were just going for a walk." I followed her because I didn't have a choice. She did have my backpack and all.

"Why don't I give you guys a ride anyway? Kevin, hop in the car."

"Wait," Kevin said. "How do you know my name?"

Jane looked up and we locked eyes.

"You were looking for us, weren't you?" I asked. The look on her face was the only answer I needed.

"Come home, Blue. Your family is worried and searching the neighborhood. You too, Kevin. Whatever you're upset about, it isn't worth losing your families over."

I shuffled my feet and looked at Kevin.

"I don't want to sleep outside," Kevin said to me quietly. "Please."

I climbed into the back of Jane's car. I could pretend that I only went home for Kevin. I could say that I was afraid Jane would call my dad if I didn't go with her. I could even admit that the darkness scared me a little more than I thought it would. But the truth was that I just really missed my family.

16

A police car was pulling away as I made my way up the driveway with Jane by my side. When we walked in the front door, relief flooded through my veins, even as my heart pounded in my chest. Technically, I had only been gone for three hours and sixteen minutes, but it felt like a whole lot longer. It felt like a lifetime.

I heard a door slam and then my father was coming toward us, his phone dangling from one ear. "We found her, Seth. Just come home." He sighed at something Seth said on the other end and then hung up.

Jane went to my dad and put her hand on his shoulder. They didn't say anything; they just stood together. He brushed a strand of hair off her forehead before she left, quietly closing the door behind her.

He was obviously *very* thankful that she found me.

My dad finally turned toward me and we stared at each

other in the hallway, neither of us moving. The dog rule doesn't apply when it's your father, which is a good thing, because I was definitely the one who looked away first.

"Do you have anything you want to say to me?" he asked. I didn't recognize the look he gave me. On the surface it looked like anger, but it was mixed with something unfamiliar.

"Do you have anything you want to say to me?" I asked him back.

He stretched his hand out toward me, then ran it through his hair. When he pulled it away, his hair stood up like freshly cut grass.

"Do you have any idea how worried I've been? Do you?" I felt a stab of guilt, but I was too angry to say anything that could possibly make him feel better. "You know what, don't say anything. Just go to your room."

"Milk," Arnie said, peeking around the corner. "Milk-milk."

"No milk," my father snapped. "Go to your room, Beulah. Now!"

I glared at my youngest brother while he blinked up at me with a goofy grin. A lump formed in my throat, but I swallowed it down and left them.

I was almost to my room when Jackson came out of nowhere.

"Where were you?" he asked. I tried to move past him, but he blocked my way. "You know what, Blue? You're selfish."

"Me? Selfish?"

"Yeah." He'd been holding a paintbrush, and now he was using it to point at me. "You're the most selfish person I know."

"You don't know what you're talking about." I tried again to push him out of the way, but he held his ground. "If you knew what I know, you wouldn't say that."

"Right. I forgot, your life is *soooo* rough. If you knew what I know, then maybe you would stop and think about someone else besides yourself."

"What's that supposed to mean?"

Jackson rolled his eyes. "What do you think happened when you ran off tonight?"

I didn't say anything.

"I'll give you a hint. Dad freaked out. Arnie was bawling. Even Seth was scared. I hope you're happy."

He squeezed himself against the wall so as not to touch me as I finished the walk to my room alone. Kota was lying on my bed and jumped down when I entered. I tried to pet him, but it seemed that even he didn't want to be around me. I watched as he padded out of my room, his tail unusually tucked down.

I changed into my softest pajamas and warmest socks, then crawled into bed. I lay there, awake, for a long time, staring at the ceiling and listening to the familiar sounds of my house. I thought about everything I now knew and what that meant about my feelings toward Arnie. I've always loved my littlest brother—I still did. But I was angry with him, too, and I didn't like how that made me feel. I knew in my head it wasn't his fault, but I was having a bit more trouble explaining that to my heart.

I heard the garage door when Seth got home and Arnie singing in the bathtub. After a while, I heard my father's muffled voice directing my brothers to bed. When the light disappeared from underneath my door, I knew everyone was in bed for the night.

My stomach was growling angrily, so I crept down the stairs toward the kitchen. I jumped when I found my dad there. He was sitting at the table in the dark, his head resting in his hands. I backed away, trying to leave as quickly and quietly as I'd entered, but it was too late. I was caught.

"Sit down, Blue."

He'd raised his head, and from the moonlight through our kitchen window, I could see tears glistening on his cheeks. I sat down across from him and waited. He rubbed his eyes and sighed.

"Are you going to talk to me about why you felt the need

to run away from home tonight?" It was hard to stay angry when I saw my father cry. "Seth already told me what you found up in the attic. I can imagine how upset and confused you must have felt. But, Blue?" He reached across the table and raised my chin so I had to look into his eyes. "It is never, ever okay to run away from home."

I felt the tears forming, and I didn't try to stop them. "I miss her, Dad. Every single day." I wiped a tear away. "But that's not why I left. It was because you lied to us. How could you do that?"

"I was afraid that if you knew the truth, you and your brothers would never accept Arnie. That you would never forgive him. He is completely innocent in all of this."

"So you decided to lie to us? Were you ever going to tell us the truth?"

My dad ran his hand through his hair. "I wanted to. I did. But then I didn't know how to start or what to say. I wanted to protect you and Seth and Jackson . . . *and* Arnie."

"But why did this happen to her?" My voice shook.

Dad stood up and poured us both small glasses of chocolate milk. It felt like an hour before he finally spoke. "Did you know that milk talks were actually your mother's idea?"

I shook my head.

"When you were a baby, sometimes Seth would act

out. He was probably just jealous of the attention you were getting. Well, for whatever reason, he always seemed to calm down if he had something to drink. Your mom was brilliant and used that time to soothe him."

He stared into his milk, and I thought about what Seth had said about Dad not being able to make eye contact when talking about Mom and the day he brought Arnie home.

"I don't know why she died, Blue. I'm sorry that I can't give you a good answer." He tried to look at me, but tears started welling in his eyes. He looked back down. "I tried to find out. Was it something we did? Something we didn't do? We read everything we could. We made our appointments. I mean, we'd already had three kids, so . . ."

I knew it couldn't be their fault; they were the best parents in the world. But I couldn't find anything to say.

Dad cleared his throat. "Sometimes mothers don't get the care they should."

I walked around the table to him, and he put his arms around me. None of this was fair. Not to him, not to me, and not to her. I wanted to be sad, but at that moment all I could feel was anger. I wanted to throw my glass of milk through the window. It was all so stupid. My mother didn't do anything wrong!

"Your mom loved you so much. She loved all of you, more than anything. Even herself. All she ever wanted was for her children to be happy and healthy. And you are." He tried to force a small smile, but he couldn't hold it. "Please forgive me for not telling you, Blue. I was only doing what I thought was best. And whatever you do, don't blame Arnie. It's not his fault."

"Milk-milk time!" I heard from the top of the stairs. A moment later, Arnie stood in the doorway, his blankie trailing behind him and grinning from ear to ear. "Milk-milk time for Arnie!"

I stood up from the table so quickly, I accidentally scraped the chair against the tile floor.

"Wait, Blue," I heard my dad call, but I was already racing back up to my room. I couldn't bear to be in the same room as Arnie. It was too much to handle. His cute little smile wasn't so cute anymore.

Well, it was still pretty cute.

But it also reminded me of my mom's, and it was all just too much right then.

Once I was back in my room, I lay on my bed and stared up at the ceiling. I thought about everything my dad had told me. The sound of my clock filled the silence.

Ticktock. Ticktock. Ticktock.

I closed my eyes and tried to sleep, but my head was still swirling with too many thoughts. I tried to think of something else to distract myself. I pictured rainbows, which made me think of crayons, which made me think of Arnie coloring at the table. I tried to count sheep, which made me think of a farm, which made me think of singing "Old MacDonald Had a Farm" with Arnie.

Ticktock. Ticktock. Ticktock.

I pulled my pillow over my head and tried to block out the sound of my clock, but it was still there. I stood up and yanked its cord out of the wall. That shut it up.

I reached under my bed and pulled out my super-secret stash of stuffed animals. I was way too old to play with them—obviously. But I could still take them out and stand them up all in a line. I mean, just to look at them.

Except Patty Panda looked kind of sad just sitting there, so I had no choice but to pick her up and hold her in my lap. And when I did that, Georgie the Llama eyed me like I'd betrayed him, so I had to hold him, too. From there it was all downhill. Norma, Nina, and Nancy all wanted love. And Ryder and Pinkie, too. Pretty soon they were all piled around me, snuggling close and warm. It's not like I wanted them or anything. It's just that they were making me feel guilty with the looks they were giving me.

I picked up Ginger, a tattered reindeer with extremely large eyes, and stared at her matted fur. She looked more loved than all the others, which is exactly as it should have been. She was my favorite. I carried Ginger everywhere the year my mom died. The year Arnie was born.

There was a soft knock on my door. I shoved as many stuffed animals as I could into the box while calling out, "Just a minute." I was sliding the whole thing back under my bed when my dad cracked the door open.

"Good night, Blue. I'm glad you're home safe." I didn't say anything. After a moment, he shut the door softly, and I listened as he walked away.

I still didn't know how to feel about everything. I was mad at my dad for lying and not trusting us with the truth. I was sad and confused that Arnie was the cause of my mother's death. I felt guilty for running away and making everyone worry. I didn't understand why Seth wasn't as upset as me. Only yesterday, everything seemed so simple. Now I didn't know what to say or how to feel about anything. All I knew was that I missed my mom more than ever.

I was about to jump back onto my bed when I saw Ginger poking out from underneath my bed. Her tiny antlers stuck out from under the bed skirt and one of her giant eyes caught the light. I must have missed placing her in the box with the others in my rush to put them all away. I picked her up and remembered a day long ago.

It was shortly after my mom died, just a normal day. The sun was out and there were no clouds in the sky, but I remember there was still a cold breeze in the air. My dad called me into the kitchen to talk, just the two of us. He gave me the stuffed animal, and I asked him why he got it for me. He told me, "Well, I guess it kind of reminded me of you. It has big beautiful brown eyes, just like you. And just like your mother."

I didn't cry when he said that. I thought at the time that I should've cried, but I didn't. Instead I went to a bookshelf that had an assortment of picture frames displayed and found the one I was looking for. I reached for the shiny silver frame and held it in my hands. I stared down at the photograph inside. My mother looked back at me, her giant brown eyes shiny from the camera's reflection. Her hair was long, longer than I remembered. She looked younger, too. But her smile was the same. And so were her eyes.

I placed Ginger on my bed and slid open the bottom drawer of my dresser. Tucked underneath my clothing was the photograph, still encased in the same silver frame. I kept it after that day and hid it in my room. If my dad noticed, he never said anything.

I climbed onto my bed, Ginger in one hand and the photo in my other. I stared at my mother's eyes like I had so many times before. Only this time, I noticed something different. It was true—I had my mother's eyes, and looking at hers was like looking into my own. But my brother had her same eyes as well.

Arnie.

I wiped away a tear and put the picture frame back in its hiding spot. Then I tiptoed down the hall to Arnie's room. He was sleeping, lying sideways across the bed with his left foot dangling off the edge. I thought about wrapping him in the blanket and rolling him down the driveway. It wasn't a terrible plan.

I went to him and pulled at his blanket, visions of him bumping along the concrete still fresh in my mind. Instead of rolling him like a burrito, I gently pulled him up, so that his head rested back on the pillow. I covered him up once again and brushed his hair off his forehead. Then I tucked Mr. Bunny Boo under his arm and crept away.

The truth was that I was a tiny bit angry with Arnie, but I was surprised to realize that I still really liked him, too. Especially when he was sleeping. And *quiet*.

I rounded the corner to my room and almost ran into Seth standing in front of my door.

"You okay?" he asked. I brushed past him, and he followed me into my room.

"Yeah," I mumbled.

"Do you hate Arnie?"

I grunted. "Not as much as I hate Jackson."

"Everyone hates Jackson," he said, and I smiled before I could stop myself.

I leaned back on my bed, and Seth sat down on the edge.

"Can I tell you something?"

I hesitated. "What?"

"We're going to be okay."

I couldn't help it. I hugged him.

When Seth stood up, he said. "You're just like her, you know." I must have looked as surprised as I felt, because he shook his head. "It's true. I knew her the longest." He picked up Ginger, and for a second it looked like he was going to hug her. Instead, he chucked the reindeer at my face and she bounced off my forehead. "Score!" He raised his arms into the air as he left my room.

I thought back to the mother I knew. The one who called me "baby girl" and rocked us all to sleep. The mom who made me strawberry soup when I had a sore throat and wore the macaroni necklace I'd made her for Mother's Day every single day for the next week. I sure didn't feel as nice as she was.

I turned off the light and snuggled into my blankets, thinking about what Seth had said. Was I really like our mom? I pondered the idea as I drifted off to sleep, Ginger held tightly in my arms. I decided she could sleep with me again just this once. I could always put her back in the box tomorrow.

17

Weeks flew by and life went on.

Right before school ended, Marley and I finished our book report on *Charlotte's Web*, and we got an A on our oral presentation. My dad got a raise at work and bought himself a shiny new laptop. Seth got a girlfriend—yep, Keira from the pool. Jackson entered an art contest and got second place for his drawing. Arnie was still speaking in third person—and Blue still thought that was weird.

Yep. Life went on.

It was finally officially summer. That, combined with it being Friday afternoon and the start of the weekend, had me practically singing as I crossed the street back home from Kevin's house.

Some people look forward to football season. Some people look forward to their bar mitzvah. Some people look forward to a hot cup of tea on a cold winter night. But me?

I look forward to the weekend. It's like an official holiday two days out of every week. I mean, I get to go to bed later, which is my absolute favorite part. I also get to sleep in later, and even if I technically don't, I still could if I really wanted to. Also, most of the time my dad is so tired by Friday night that he just orders pizza. The weekend is a nonstop party, if you ask me.

And this particular weekend was getting upgraded to THE BEST WEEKEND EVER.

On Sunday afternoon, a limousine was going to pick us up from our house and take us to a fabulous hotel. Normally, the winners of the *Family Tree* contest would have been flown to California, but since we already live there and San Diego is only two hours away from Hollywood, they decided to send a car for us. That's the fancy way to say it, I think.

"We will send a car for you," they said.

"That would be lovely," my dad said.

Then we all jumped up and down, hands together, with our mouths open wide in silent screams. A real-life limousine!

Once we arrive and check into the hotel, we'll get to swim or do whatever we want. On the next day, we're going to visit the set of my favorite TV show, *Family Tree*. And then, as if all of that isn't enough, I am really, truly, legitimately going to meet London Malloy, the greatest actress ever and my soon-to-be new best friend. I'd never met anyone—besides my brothers—who had lost their mother, like me. London and I would have so much to talk about, I didn't even know where to start.

Unfortunately, the prize was only for a family of four, and we were a family of *five*. This meant one of us couldn't go. Luckily, Arnie didn't realize what he'd be missing, so he wasn't upset at all when my dad told him he'd be staying home. And I don't blame him. If it wasn't my favorite TV show we'd be visiting and if it wasn't my favorite actress we'd be meeting, I'd want to stay home, too. It was all on account of Uncle Harley and how much we all love him.

Uncle Harley is my mom's brother. His real name is Eugene, but like me, no one ever called him by his for-reals name. This is because he doesn't look like a Eugene *at all*. He's a giant—he is the tallest man I know—and he is burly and loud with a deep voice that rumbles like thunder. His hair is so gray it's almost white, and it sticks out all around him and mixes into his beard so you don't know where his head hair begins and his beard hair ends.

The first time Arnie saw a picture of Santa Claus, he pointed and said, "Uncle Harley!" I kind of had to agree. If Santa had tattoos and rode a Harley, then my uncle would definitely be him. This wasn't only because they looked so much alike, although they both had that red-cheeked jolly look about them. It was also because my Uncle Harley was one of the nicest and kindest people I had ever met. Really. He would risk his life to save a baby kitten. Well, anybody would save a baby kitten. But he would also risk his life to save *Jackson*—so that's saying something.

I didn't need the motorcycle in the driveway to tell me my uncle was already there—I could hear his booming voice all the way from the street. I burst through the front door and followed the sound of his laughter. It took me into the backyard, where the rest of my family was already gathered at the patio table, everyone except for Arnie. It was still his nap time, so he was probably upstairs sleeping.

Uncle Harley was front and center. He looked the exact same as every other time I'd seen him: black leather vest, jeans, and studded boots. With a mess of wild hair, of course.

"I'm so glad you're here! I thought you weren't coming until later tonight," I said. Uncle Harley wrapped me up in a giant bear hug.

"The drive was faster than I thought. Besides, I can't pass up one of your dad's delicious home-cooked meals."

Jackson and I exchanged a look. I don't think either one of us wanted to expose the truth about our dad's cooking skills.

"He's joking," my dad said, ruffling Jackson's hair. "He's had my cooking before."

I wandered inside to pour myself a glass of iced tea and then went back outside to sit with my family. Seth was talking to Uncle Harley about surfing.

"It's all about that perfect wave, you know?" Seth said, demonstrating with his hands. "It's like a roller coaster ride on water. I can't wait to show you when we get there."

"Get where?" I asked.

"We're going to the beach this afternoon." My dad looked down at his watch. "Actually, we should probably start getting our stuff together. Jackson, did you put the sunscreen back in the cabinet?"

"What? Wait a second. Uncle Harley just got here and now we're all leaving to go to the beach?"

"That's right," my dad said. "And I need you to make sure Arnie feeds his turtle before we go."

Shocked, my mouth dropped wide open. I glanced at the tree in the corner of the backyard that was Fruit Ninja's home. Even though I only looked for less than half a second, I realized it was enough to give me away. Now my dad knew that I knew that he knew that I knew.

"You knew this whole time?" I asked him incredulously.

"Did you really think I wouldn't notice a turtle living in our yard?" My dad shook his head. "Amateurs."

I went to wake Arnie from his nap, but he wasn't in his room. After a couple minutes, I finally found him sitting under the dining-room table, crashing his toy trucks together. "You need to feed your turtle before we go to the beach," I told him, leaning down so he could see my face. "Try giving him a banana."

Arnie crawled out from under the table and left, so I made my way toward my room to change into my bathing suit. I was halfway up the stairs when I heard Arnie crying out.

"Fruit Ninja's gone!" he howled between tears.

"What do you mean?" I asked, hurrying back down. He ran into my arms, so I held him tight against me.

"Arnie looked all over, but he's not there," he said, the words muffled by my shirt. "He's gone!"

"It's okay, Arnie. I'm sure he's just hiding somewhere." I gave him a squeeze and then pulled him away so I could look down at him. "Come on. I'll help you find him."

He followed me toward the back door, hiccupping and sniffling as he tried to calm down.

I wasn't too worried, as I was sure the turtle was just hiding somewhere. His enclosure was pretty big, and there were lots of places he could tuck himself into. I held Arnie's hand as we trekked out into the backyard, but Arnie was right. When we got to his special tree, Fruit Ninja was nowhere to be found.

"See?" Another giant tear fell from Arnie's eyes, but I could see he was trying so hard to be brave. "He's gone."

"It's okay, Arnie. We'll find him." I hoped. "Let's look around the yard."

We looked everywhere. We searched through the grass and bushes, under the deck and over the rocks. We checked the front yard and the side of the house. Fruit Ninja must've been a real-life ninja, because we couldn't find that crazy turtle anywhere.

"I'm sorry, Arnie. I don't know where else to look."

"Mrs. Atchinson? Arnie found him in her garden. Maybe he went back."

I gazed at the back of Mrs. Atchinson's fence and thought about it. I mean, it was possible that the little turtle made his way back over there. I looked back at Arnie and saw his eyes light up with the renewed hope that Fruit Ninja could still be found. I knew then that I had to at least try.

"Okay, this is what we do. Since, technically, you're not allowed in her garden, you can keep watch. I'll hop over the fence and look for him. Where was he again?"

"Next to the peas."

"Arnie! You were eating the sugar snaps, weren't you?"

"No."

"Arnie . . ."

He sighed. "Arnie ate the peas."

I put the vegetable dilemma to the side and focused on finding Fruit Ninja. Mrs. Atchinson lived directly behind us, so the backsides of our yards shared a fence. Arnie made sure no one was looking while I climbed over the fence. As soon as I dropped down into her yard, I raced over to her vegetable garden.

I pawed through her lettuce and tomatoes, searching for Fruit Ninja. I lifted leaves and shuffled through the dirt, but I couldn't find him anywhere. I was standing up to leave when I heard something next to me. Arnie was crouched down next to the sugar snap peas.

"Arnie! I told you to stay on the other side of the fence and keep watch. And for goodness' sake, quit eating the poor woman's peas!"

"Arnie's not," he whispered, still staring down at the ground. I went over to see what he was looking at and gasped. Arnie found Fruit Ninja . . . and his family!

"Arnie! You found three Fruit Ninjas!" I laughed, but Arnie wasn't smiling.

"Arnie doesn't know who he is. They all look the same. How can Arnie bring him back?" He looked so small standing there.

I didn't say anything. I wasn't sure how to explain to

Arnie that if there were other turtles there, we should leave him. The turtles probably depended on one another. Maybe they even loved one another.

As it turned out, I didn't have to say anything.

"He looks happy." Arnie raised his determined little chin, even as it trembled and his eyes filled with tears again. "He should stay here."

I looked at Arnie. I mean, I really paid attention to him. He had tried so hard to be a true turtle hero, even if what he did was wrong. I watched as he silently wiped the tears off his cheeks. It made my heart ache for him. I knew how hard it was for him to leave Fruit Ninja there in the garden, because I knew how much he loved that silly turtle. I was really proud of him for doing the right thing all on his own. No animal should be taken out of its habitat.

"Maybe we can come and visit him sometimes," I said gently.

Arnie was quiet and didn't say anything. Then he flew toward me and wrapped his arms around my waist. I hugged him close while he cried. After a while, he started to slow down. He wiped his snot on my shirt and I didn't even say anything mean.

"You ready to go?" I asked when he let go of me. I glanced at Mrs. Atchinson's house, envisioning the old lady chasing us out of her yard with a cane. We needed to get out of there. Arnie nodded and reached for my hand.

"Blue?"

"Yes, Arnie?"

"Arnie's happy you were here when Arnie had to say goodbye."

"Me, too." I gave his hand a squeeze.

"You're a good big sister."

I love you, too, Arnie, I thought to myself. But out loud I said, "Last one to put on their bathing suit is a rotten egg!"

I let him have a good head start, which in brother-sister speak is the same thing as saying *I love you.* I wanted him to know it, even if I didn't say it out loud.

18

Uncle Harley's arrival meant only one thing: Summer was in full effect, and the time had come to visit the set of *Family Tree*. My trip of a lifetime had finally arrived! I could barely contain my excitement and wiggled my butt like my pants were on fire.

When our super-fancy limo pulled up to the hotel, I leaned my head out the window and gasped. The size of the hotel took my breath away. The main building was shaped like an *L* and was about a million stories high. It had revolving glass doors with concrete pillars next to concrete statues and a giant fountain that lit up the entrance with its rainbow-colored lights. Another smaller tower of rooms stood next to the main building, and in between them was an enormous pool the size of Alaska.

And I couldn't wait to swim from one end of it to the other.

Our super-fancy limo driver opened our door, and then a super-fancy man in a green suit took all of our luggage, so I didn't even have to carry anything. Once inside, my brothers and I waited while our dad spoke to a woman behind a tall counter, and then we took an elevator up to our room. It took forever to get there because it was pretty high up. It also took forever because there was a really obnoxious kid—whose name rhymes with *Macksfin*—who thought it would be funny to push extra buttons so that the elevator stopped six different times on the way up. I distracted my dad while Seth punched that certain obnoxious kid. When the elevator finally stopped on our floor and the doors slid open, I was the first one out, grateful for the fresh air.

The key they gave us looked like a credit card, and my dad let me use it to open the door. Jackson got mad because he wanted to try it first, so I *gently reminded* him that sometimes it's better not to be so selfish and to think of others. I also *very nicely* suggested that he try and not be a giant baby for the entire trip, as it wasn't very fun for the rest of us. And even though I was only looking out for my father's best interest, for some reason I got in trouble for saying that.

I know. Weird, right?

After my dad and I had a mini milk-talk without the milk and I was *gently reminded* to keep my opinions to myself, I finally got a chance to look around the place. It was like a real-life palace! Just like the outside, there were giant pillars on the inside next to every single set of doors—and there were a lot of them. There were two separate bedrooms and two separate bathrooms. And every single room had a TV, even the bathrooms, which was really weird and really cool at the same time. The TVs in the sitting area and the bedrooms were bigger than our biggest TV, and one of the bathrooms had a bathtub that was so big, I bet a baby T. rex could've taken a bath in it.

My dad said he'd never been inside a hotel room this fancy.

I said we should get TVs for all of our bathrooms at home.

Seth said he hoped the minibar was free while opening a bag of chips.

Jackson said he could smell my feet. (Guess who got the mini milk-talk without the milk that time?)

As soon as our suitcases were brought up to our room, I changed into my bathing suit, eager to *S-W-I-M*. My brothers did the same and then my dad took us down to the pool. I think he was eager to *N-A-P*, because he found a shady spot underneath a tree, and instead of reading the book he'd brought down with him, he opened it up and used it to cover his face. But if he wanted to sleep, that was fine by me. As long as I could dip my princess toes into that amazing pool of awesomeness, I was a very happy girl.

We spent the whole afternoon swimming, and my brothers never once left me out. We played Who Can Hold Their Breath The Longest and Seth won. We played Who Can Swim The Fastest and Seth won. We played Who Can Jump Farthest and Seth won that, too, but I didn't even care. There were five slides and inflatable tubes and a wave pool. In between all that losing, I was having the best time of my life.

The next morning I insisted on taking a shower even though I'd taken one right before bed the night before. I used the hair dryer in the bathroom and then I brushed my hair until it was soft and shiny. I put on a navy-blue dress, which went perfectly with my red sparkle shoes, and my grown-up gold-star earrings. I looked in the mirror and thought I looked very sophisticated, which was good, because I really wanted to make an amazing first impression.

The same super-fancy limo picked us up and took us to the *Family Tree* set, where we would watch the filming of an episode. We had to sign in at the desk and they gave us each a badge with our photo on it that we wore like a necklace. Then a woman with a headset and a clipboard told us to follow her through two sets of doors until, before

I knew it, we were standing in front of a set. It was London Malloy's living room.

And there, sitting on the couch, was London Malloy herself!

My stomach swarmed with butterflies and my heart pounded in my chest. London was nodding at the director as he gave her stage directions for the next scene. She must've understood what he said, because a moment later he moved back behind the camera.

"Action!" he called out, and then they ran the scene.

London Malloy skipped onto the set with her dog trailing behind her. We weren't supposed to make any sound, so when he galloped across the stage with his tongue hanging out the side of his mouth, I had to try hard not to giggle. She crouched down to pet him before she spoke.

"Aww, Uncle Bradley, why can't I take Rocky to the dog park?"

"Because it looks like it's going to rain soon. Besides, I have a new recipe for chicken parmesan, and I thought you could help me make it tonight."

Then London Malloy's brother, Kyle, popped through the door, and he was even cuter in real life than he was on television. When he smiled, a dimple appeared in his left cheek, and the sight of it made my heart flutter.

"It's okay, London, I walked Rocky this morning. Hey,

would you mind helping me with my math homework? Even though I'm older, you're still so much better than me."

London Malloy pulled him in for a hug, and for a moment, the siblings stayed that way, smiling as they embraced.

"Cut!" the director yelled.

Instantly, London Malloy shook out of Kyle's hug, but he wasn't upset by her force. It looked like he couldn't get away from her fast enough.

Kyle called out to the director. "I'm confused. Why would she be better than me at math? It doesn't make any sense. My character is a science champion."

London Malloy rolled her eyes. "Because you're not the star of the show. *I am!*"

Kyle must have snapped back, because it sounded like they were bickering as London followed him offstage. I stood in shock, not really sure how I felt about watching them fight like that. I looked up at my dad, and he tried to smile.

"Well, that was certainly interesting," he said.

"What just happened?" Jackson asked, looking bewildered.

The lady with the headset and clipboard approached us. "Excuse me, but can you please follow me?" We made our way back the way we came, but when we got to the main hallway, we turned down a different corridor. "These are the private dressing rooms for all our actors and actresses, as well as the hair and makeup room all our stars share."

She guided us through a large door into a brightly lit salon. Mirrors and lights lined the walls, with chairs set up for each station. Two women and a man stood ready to go, makeup brushes and combs waiting in their hands.

"London Malloy will join you shortly. She is—"

"She is *what*, Jennifer?"

The headset lady jumped at the sound of London Malloy's voice and almost dropped her clipboard. London slinked into the room and sat down at one of the makeup stations.

"Nothing, Ms. Malloy. I was only going to say that you were getting a drink of water." She fidgeted nervously. "I'd like to introduce you to," she looked down at her clipboard, "Beulah Warren. She won the art contest and is here to—"

"How many times do I have to tell you people that I do not wear headbands? They make me look like a baby *and I am not a baby*!" She pulled off the headband she'd been wearing and threw it across the room.

"No one thinks you're a baby," Jennifer tried to tell her, but London wasn't listening.

I felt a trickle of sweat run down my back as I watched her behavior. My brothers were silent, which was a relief, because if they'd said anything, I would've started crying. I felt devastated trying to process this new London Malloy, so different than the one I'd been expecting. My hands were shaking from the shock of it all. I held them close against me so no one would notice.

London Malloy wasn't the person I thought she was. I moved closer to my dad and reached for his hand. I suddenly felt very alone. Here I thought she was someone I wanted to be friends with. Best friends. The truth was that I didn't want to be in the same room as her. I wasn't even sure if I wanted her to know anymore that my mom had died, too.

Rocky the dog bounded through the doors and tried to jump onto London's lap.

"Ew! Get this smelly dog away from me!" London Malloy turned to a tall woman who had appeared in the doorway. She had jet-black hair pulled back into a bun at the nape of her neck. "I thought you said we could write the dog off the show? Can't we just say he died somehow?"

I gasped. Why would London Malloy want Rocky off the show? He ran over to me and sniffed my hand. I bent down to pet him, and he sat down next to me, leaning into my side. Jackson crouched down next to me and scratched him behind his ears.

London Malloy kept on. "Or send him to a dog farm. I don't care what they do, I just want him gone!"

Everything she said was like word vomit—nasty and foul—and with each word that came out of her mouth, my hopes and dreams drifted further away.

A whistle came from the hallway outside the room and Rocky hopped up, darting out the door. With the adorable dog out of the way, there was no other distraction from the horror of London Malloy, former best-friend-in-training.

The woman with the bun said, "It's all right, darling. I will speak to whoever I need to and have that filthy canine removed immediately."

"That's what you always say, Mother, but that dog is still here. It's like you're completely useless." London Malloy turned back to the mirror and fussed with her hair. "Honestly, Mother, can't you figure out how to do something as simple as getting rid of a dog?"

London Malloy's mother was alive.

And London Malloy was a terrible person.

"Get me out of here," I whispered. I couldn't bear to watch her for another second.

"London, you know I don't like when you talk to me like that." Her mother tried to touch her shoulder, but London jerked her arm away.

"Then don't be stupid, Mother."

"Get me out of here," I whispered a little louder. It was like I'd suddenly forgotten how to speak, and my tongue felt thick inside my mouth. I tried to swallow. I tried to breathe.

The woman with the headset, Jennifer, whispered something in London Malloy's ear. She looked around the room until her eyes settled on me. Then she looked back at Jennifer and asked, loud enough for me to hear, "Beulah? What kind of name is that?"

I found my voice.

I pointed at London Malloy, my insides on fire from all the rage that had been building. "You are disgusting. How dare you talk to your own mother like that! My mom named me Beulah and it is a perfectly fine name. You are a fraud and a liar and I can't believe I actually wanted you to be my friend!" I turned away from her and looked up at my dad, pleading with my eyes. I needed him to understand. "Get me out of here," I said quietly, just to him this time.

He understood.

He marched me out of that room, my brothers right behind us. Jennifer scanned her clipboard, then hollered after us, "Wait. It's not time to leave yet. You still get a photograph with London Malloy and . . ."

I followed my dad through the maze of hallways until we were back at the front entrance. The last thing I did before walking out of those doors was take off my badge and throw it down on the ground. I was secretly happy when my brothers did the same.

Luckily, our super-fancy limo was waiting for us, and I climbed right in.

"I can't believe you yelled like that!" Seth said.

"You were awesome!" Jackson was smiling big.

For the first time since I saw London Malloy, I felt like I could breathe again, which actually wasn't a good thing. Breathing also meant that I could finally get enough air to cry properly, and so that's what I did. My dad put his arm around me, and I buried my face into his shoulder.

"That woman was her mother . . . and the way she was talking to her . . ." I couldn't say anything more through my tears.

"I know, kiddo. I know." My dad patted my head.

He didn't *really* know how I felt, he couldn't possibly, but I appreciated him trying.

Then I remembered the two smelly, annoying, bother-some, loud, obnoxious brothers of mine that actually *did* know what I was feeling. I locked eyes with Seth.

"You okay?" he asked me.

I nodded, wiping my face and snot on our dad's sleeve when he wasn't looking.

"Hey, Blue?" Jackson said.

"Yeah?"

"You're cool."

I tried to smile, but I knew it was plastic. My eyes felt as empty as they did wet.

"For real," Jackson went on, "I could never say all that stuff. You were . . . What's that word? Phen . . . phenan . . . phemom . . ."

"Phenomenal?" Seth said.

"That's it," Jackson said, snapping his fingers. "You were phenomenal."

My dad squeezed my shoulders and whispered into my ear, "I'm proud of you, Blue. Do you know that?"

I stared out the window as the busy city flew past us in a blur. Was I really finally phenomenal at something? And if so, what exactly was I phenomenal at? Yelling at somebody I had admired when I woke up this morning? Defending my mother's choice in names when the truth was even I disliked the name Beulah? Or maybe I was phenomenal because I allowed myself to think that I could ever have anything in common with someone like London Malloy.

We got back to the hotel, and my dad went with the boys back down to the pool. I stayed in the hotel room and curled up on the window seat, happy for a little alone time. The window jutted out of the wall so that I was surrounded on all three sides by clear glass. It felt like I was sitting in the middle of the world.

I gazed into the bright blue sky and thought about my mom. I didn't close my eyes this time, trying to see her in my mind. The fading was happening faster now, so I'd stopped doing that a while ago. Every time I tried to picture her, she got more and more blurry. It was like the ocean chipping away at a sandcastle. Each crash of the wave took a few tiny grains of sand, until there was nothing left but a hole where there used to be a kingdom.

I knew that I wasn't going to remember everything about my mom, and I was starting to realize that the memories I did have probably weren't going to last forever. I remembered her beautiful red fingernails, but I couldn't tell you if our hands were the same shape. I remembered curling up in her lap watching *The Wizard of Oz*, but I couldn't recall if we sang along to the songs.

It didn't mean that I didn't love her; I loved her more than there were stars in the sky. It just meant I couldn't remember her with my eyes. Or with my brain. I remembered my mother the only way I knew how. With my heart.

I think that's how people are truly meant to be remembered anyway.

Pounding footsteps echoed down the hall, followed by muffled voices on the other side of the door. The doorknob rattled wildly a second later.

"Hurry up. How hard can it be to unlock?"

"Stop it, Seth. Get out of my way."

I hopped down from the window seat and waited for Tweedledee and Tweedledum to enter. Even after they got the door open, they were still pushing and shoving each other as they paraded back into the room.

"Dad wants you to come down to the pool," Seth said. "He said to tell you that you should be with your family."

"Plus Dad promised that if we got you to go down there, he would get us all ice cream," Jackson said.

"Well, you're out of luck, because I'm not going anywhere." I crossed my arms over my chest.

"Come on," Seth said. "Come to the pool with us. Tell you what, I'll even teach you how to dive."

I just looked at him, remembering the day at Arnie's swimming lesson when he *did* teach me how to dive. He still didn't know.

Seth puffed out his chest. "I've been surfing since I was four years old. If anyone can teach you, it's me."

Jackson said, "If she can even be taught. Maybe she'll never be able to dive." I gave him the same look I gave Seth.

"I bet I can dive the first time I try." I tried not to sound too confident.

"Yeah right," Jackson said at the same time Seth snorted.

"If you really think that, then you won't be scared of a little friendly wager, right?"

My eyebrows shot into the air. "What kind of wager?"

"I'll bet your ice cream that you can't do it on the first try," Jackson said.

"Me, too," Seth said. "I want in on that bet."

It was like taking candy from a baby. Two babies, actually. Big dumb ice cream–less babies.

I clarified the rules one more time, just to be sure. "Okay, so if I manage to dive on my first try, I get both of your ice creams?"

"Yes, but more importantly, if you don't, we get *yours*." Seth smiled big like he'd already won.

I changed into my bathing suit, reached for my towel, and then followed them out the door. I almost laughed out loud at my sudden realization. I didn't need London Malloy to be my best friend. I certainly didn't need her to understand me and my life. What I'd been looking for was already right in front of me. We stepped onto the elevator and Jackson started pushing all of the buttons. So Seth punched him.

And it was while watching Jackson get walloped that I understood how lucky I was. I had three obnoxious, loud-chewing, sister-pestering, sticky, smelly brothers who I kind of enjoyed most of the time. (Some more than others.) And I was pretty sure they actually liked me, too. (Some more than others.) I could get through anything, as long as I had my wacky family by my side. I wouldn't trade them for all the ice cream in the world.

And that was saying something.

ACKNOWLEDGMENTS

First off, a special thanks to my amazing agent, Steven Chudney. Thank you for working so hard to find a home for Blue and for believing in me! Your sarcastic wit makes me smile always. I'm so glad we chose each other for this magical journey!

To Brett Duquette, you have taught me so much along the way. Thank you for taking a chance on this newbie author, and for championing this book. Your knowledge, expertise, creativity, and flat-out talent are such gifts! I feel so lucky to have been able to work with you! To the other incredible people buzzing about at Little Bee, thank you for all of your effort and hard work! Kayla Overbey, Dave Barrett, Shimul Tolia, Paul Crichton, and Natalie Padberg Bartoo . . . none of this could have happened without each and every one of you. (And for Kayla . . . an extra-special thank you from Fruit Ninja!)

I had many wonderful teachers growing up, but Mr. and Mrs. Jones went above and beyond. I've waited a long time to say this: Thank you for seeing this young girl when no one else did. Mr. Jones, you made me want to learn in a way no one else ever had before. And Mrs. Jones, you have a heart of gold. I'm a better person because of the two of you.

Thank you to my RSS family! Sara and Aaron Hoffman, thank you for showing me what it means to be part of a big family, even if it's a little hard for me sometimes. To Kim Trotter, thank you for always checking my crazy. To Stephanie Gonzales, thank you for always telling it like it is. To Jessica Beuten, thank you for being the sweetest person I've ever met. And to all three of you, thank you for taking the time to read *Blue* and be a part of the process!

To Annika, my forever friend. Thank you for a lifetime of friendship. I admire you and love you more than you will ever know. And to Mike, for being the best friend a girl could ever ask for. You never stopped believing in me. Just know, I will never stop appreciating you.

Hunter, Emma and Haiden, always believe in yourself! You can do anything you set your mind to, so dream big, cutie-pies!

To Brooklyn and Dylan, may you always keep me on my toes and be the reason I smile daily. You are the absolute brightest stars, and I feel so lucky I get to watch you shine!

To my babe, my full house, and my partner in crime, Jake. You are my dream come true and my happily ever after. Thank you for that first night we met . . . for spinning me under the twinkling lights and for completely taking my breath away. And thank you for every day since then. There's no one else I want by my side in this life. Always and forever, baby.

And lastly, to my Samantha Noel—you are the true love of my life and my absolute favorite person in the whole world. You never cease to amaze me with your creativity, kindness, integrity, and incredible beauty both inside and out. I am beyond proud to be your mother, and I am honored that I get to call you friend. I love you, sweet girl.